My Girl

Got a

Girlfriend

By
James Tanner

My Girl Got a Girlfriend
Copyright © 2011 by James G. Tanner, Jr.

Editor/Typesetter: Carla M. Dean (www.ucanmarkmyword.com)
Cover Design: Oddball Dsgn

Printed in the United States of America

First Edition

ISBN: 13-digit: 978-0-9797094-1-8

Copies can be ordered by sending $15.00 plus $5.00 for shipping and handling to:

Park Bench Entertainment, Inc.
c/o James Tanner
P.O. Box 7223
Silver Spring, MD 20907

Acknowledgements

I want to give all praise to God for blessing me with the intelligence to write this book and for guiding me in the right direction and making all this possible.

I want to thank my mother and father, Barbara Tanner and James Tanner, my brother Micheal Tanner, my children Marja', Drake and Damari, my aunt Kim Oliver- Parker, Alardo Parker, Keisha Parker, Melissa Lockhart and the rest of the Lockhart family, MC Lucky, Moka, Babii, Nonchalant, DJ C Sharpe, Butta and Bodacious Ent., Blade and Blade Ent., Editor Carla M. Dean, Mz. Vicki, OOHZEE, Robert "Shaka" Mercer, Lil' Chris and the Downing family Tommy Lay, David "Lucan" Bailey, Curtis Smith, Carl Hunter, Cousin Nicky, Cousin Crystal, Cousin Peaches, Donald Boone, Fat Boy, Darrell King, Cassandra Riddick aka "Smoochie", Frank Sudds, Yolanda, Tunnie and Veda thanks for the kids, Cousin Mikey, Cousin Ashley, Lushy Lush, Amazin, Angela of 21st, Jetta, Mecca Reccio, Taresa Sledge, Tonya aka Ms Bossy, Ms.Tiesha "Ty" Lawrence, Gail Williams, Kurt at 15 and C, Ronald Blue, Jerome Bradshaw, Shermon Bunch, Lonnie, DJ, Smokey B, Smoke D, Veronica Green, Uncle Steve, Aunt Wanda, Aunt Mary and Donald, Andre, Skip, Tay, Mya Macoy, Viva and Secret Weapon Ent. Vernon and Wilmont Rush, Chantal Mason, Cousin Shantel and Lil' Sam, Cousin Crystal Martin, Ray Allen, William Johnson, Valarie Lewis, Charnika Edwards, Tuffy, French Kiss, Beautiful, Ladonna Mitchell, Ke Ke the Barber, Beaver, my lawyer Brain McDaniels, Broadway and Chyna Black, my graphic artist Davida Baldwin, Don Scott, Walter Brown, Donald "Donnie" Thomas, Margret and the

James Tanner

Skylark crew, Derrick Pumphry, my entertainment attorney Fred Samuels, Joanne Hudson, Karen Gray Houston and Fox 5 News, Sam Ford and Channel 7 News Center, my five thousand Facebook friends, My Girl Got A Girlfriend Facebook fans, my YouTube page friends, the whole LGBT Community, Reflexxx, Leo Gordy, Marlon, my taxman, Bernard and XII Restaurant, Olan, Fox, Ricky Seafers, Sam Foster, Shawanna and Angie, Tomoni, Sadae and Bay Bay, Mattie Reed, and all the new friends I've met thus far and in my future. If I left anyone out, please remember that you are special, too.

Check me out at:
www.facebook.com/bigmoneyjames
www.youtube.com/mygirlgotagirlbook
www.youtube.com/jamestannerfilms
www.parkbenckentertainment.weebly.com

You can also email me at investors4film@yahoo.com.

My Girl

Got a

Girlfriend

Chapter 1
THE WAY IT ALL GOT STARTED

"It was December 31, 1985, with about fifty-nine seconds left in the year. All you could hear was the sound of people cheering while running up and down the street screaming, 'Happy New Year!'" Momma said as she reminisced about the night I was born.

"The sound of gunshots could be heard everywhere," Dad added from across the room.

It is said that many people lose their lives on New Year's Eve, but this time, a life was given. I was born at midnight on January 1, 1986, on the neighborhood crackhouse floor. Not only were my proud parents two people who bring so much purpose and meaning to each other in many ways, but they were also gay.

My father was a transvestite, who was definitely known for his beauty. He stood about 5-feet, 6-inches tall and weighed about 145 pounds. His measurements were 36-24-36 on a shapely, caramel frame. Many men who thought he was a woman had given out their telephone numbers, e-mail addresses, and business cards to him. However, there were many others who knew he was a man and still wanted to be with him. Even though he was a homosexual male, he was one of the top-paid male prostitutes on the track. Most of the drug dealers in the neighborhood respected him for what he did to get paid, but on the down low, many of them paid my father for sex, too. On many occasions, my father was arrested, and sometimes he would get into altercations because of him being transgender.

My mother, on the other hand, was a straight-up dyke. She didn't take any shit, and the bitch could fight her ass off. During that time, she was a very dominant woman who believed in living her life to the fullest. When I was around ten years of age, I would often hear her say, "I got the best of both worlds in one package: a man and a woman. And me? I'm the baddest muthafucka all in one."

Momma stood 5-feet, 10-inches, weighed about 180 pounds, and had a muscular frame. Most people mistook her for a man because she would cut off all her hair until she was bald, and she would dress in extra large black sweatpants, a hoodie,

8

Timberland boots, and fitted baseball caps turned backwards. Sometimes, her crotch area would bulge if she were wearing her 13-inch strap-on dick that she used to fuck her many girlfriends. She'd even fuck my father with it. It was during those times that I would often hear him scream out in pain in the middle of the night.

"Shut the fuck up, bitch, and put some more baby oil on my dick. I want more of that asshole," Momma would yell.

I guess you can say she was an institutionalized bitch. She stayed locked up. If she weren't in the D.C. jail, it was the federal penitentiary for her. I remember when she would tell my father some of her jailhouse stories.

"I hit this bitch in the head with an ax the second week I was on the compound when I got locked up. Bitch gonna holla at a broad that I was trying to fuck the day I hit the jailhouse. The broad was so phat that I wanted to suck the bitch's pussy and her ass at the same time," Momma said, while watching my father put on a pair of thongs and a short skirt that only covered a small portion of his big, heart-shaped ass.

Momma and Daddy were good partners when it came to making ends meet. He would go out on the track to sell his ass, and she would walk up and down the block being his pimp.

"Get my money, bitch! Like two and two, make them niggas do what they do—spend that money. Bitch, get my money!"

Momma screamed as she walked behind my homosexual dad.

As a child, I really didn't understand the situation nor did I understand the roles they had to play to keep the rent paid and food in the house. I didn't even understand that my household was run differently than others. However, I did notice that my parents were a little different than my friends' parents.

For the next eleven years, I went on the track with my mother to help watch Dad's back and to get the money from him as fast as he made it. I even had to walk up and down the block and scream at Dad just like Momma had to do, but no matter who it is you're dealing with, business is business. At least that's what Momma taught me.

"Get my money, bitch! Hurry up! Get my money now, bitch!" I yelled as my father got into a car with his first trick of the night.

"Dontaye! Hey, Dontaye!" my mother screamed from across the street.

As she continued to call my name, I looked and saw her fighting two well-known undercover police officers that patrol the northwest area of Washington, D.C. Officer Burrell was a dark-skinned cop with a shinny, bald head. He stood about 6'9" and weighed about 300 pounds—all muscle. You could look at Officer Burrell and tell that the only thing he did all fucking day was lift weights.

Now, Officer Smith was a slender, white cop who stood about 5'11" and weighed about 145 pounds. Officer Smith was a natural redhead with lots of freckles on his face. The pimps and male prostitutes gave Officer Smith the nickname Red Devil because he was a corrupt cop that had a reputation for planting illegal drugs on people, assaulting people and robbing them for their money and jewelry, and even killing people if he was hired to do so.

I ran across the street to see what was going on between my mother and the two officers.

"Hey, stop hitting my peoples!" I yelled, while approaching Officers Burrell and Smith. As I pushed Officer Red Devil off of my mother, he pulled out his .9mm service weapon from its holster and pointed it at my forehead.

"Move back, sir. I said, move your ass back!" Officer Red Devil said between his gritted white teeth.

As I stepped back a few feet with my hands high in the air, my mother and Officer Burrell fought like two pit bulls fighting for dear life. Suddenly, Officer Burrell dropped to his knees while holding on to his penis, and my mother started running down the block. Officer Red Devil ran after her for several blocks, but my mother evasively outran him. I ran in the opposite direction, later meeting her at the Honeycomb Hideout where my father, my mother, and I called home.

For about six months, Momma decided to lay low and not be seen on the strip. She felt I should step up to the plate and run things for a while. I had just turned seventeen years old and had no problem with it, because for the past seven years, I had been in training. It was now time to get paid from my experience with the game.

The first day I hit the track, Officers Burrell and Red Devil pulled up on me as I stood outside a Chinese restaurant on 12th and N Streets in northwest D.C. It was about eleven o'clock on a Saturday night, and all of the male prostitutes were strolling up and down the track making that money. They were either jumping in and out of cars or going in and out of the alley.

"Hey, young man, put your hands behind your head and get on your knees," Officer Burrell said as he jumped out an unmarked police car.

"Who was that fuckin' jerk that ran that day?" Officer Red Devil yelled, while putting handcuffs on me.

"One of my informants told me it was your mother. Is that true?" Officer Burrell questioned.

"I don't know what you're talking about, sir," I answered.

"Bitch motherfucker, that bitch kicked me in the nuts!" Officer Burrell screamed, then slapped me so hard that I fell to the concrete.

Officer Red Devil laughed as he gave my mother the

nickname Rabbit.

"What's your name boy?" he asked.

"Dontaye, Officer Red Devil," I responded.

"You tell Rabbit that we're looking for her ass. You hear me, boy?"

"Yes, sir. Yes, sir. I hear you, sir," I said as Officer Burrell removed the handcuffs from my wrists. Then they got back into the unmarked police car and drove off.

I was fucked up about them dogging me out the way they did, but I had a feeling I would be having more run-ins with them in the days to come.

Since I've been on the track, many things have changed for the better. My father earned the nickname Creamy from one of his many customers, or should I say from one of his regular clientele. Creamy told me that one of the young drug dealers in the neighborhood, who is on the down low, rated his sex a 10, and that was on a scale from 1 to 10, with 10 being the greatest he's ever had. Creamy said a lot of the young dudes that sell drugs on the corner are on the down low and still go home to their women like they only ride one side of the fence. For instance, there is one particular dude that hangs out on the corner and talks that thug shit like he's a true gangster. Actually, that same youngin' said that Creamy's ass feels better than pussy. As a matter of fact, he claims it gets just as wet or wetter. Creamy also said the youngin' had a very huge penis that he liked to have sucked until the head swelled up to the size of a tennis ball.

"At times, the youngin' would slam that huge cucumber-sized dick down my throat so hard that it would make snot run from my nose and actually bring tears to my eyes," Creamy said as he started walking towards a car that seemed to be a potential trick.

As I stood on the corner near the Chinese joint, two known pimps walked up the block. Sonny Redz and Johnny Black were two of the flashiest pimps in Washington, D.C. Sonny Redz, an old timer from back in the day, was a tall, slender man with the whitest teeth I had ever seen. At times, I would see Sonny Redz in very colorful outfits. You might see him dressed in an all red or all green suit with a pair of alligator shoes to match. Whenever you saw Sonny Redz, he was always clean and sharp.

Johnny Black was a lot different than Sonny Redz. Johnny Black was much younger, much bigger, and much louder. He stood about six-feet, nine-inches tall and weighed about 365 pounds. Johnny Black would put you in mind of Suge Knight.

Sonny Redz and Johnny Black only pimped women that made them lots of money. They wouldn't waste their time pimpin' a bum bitch at all.

As Sonny Redz and Johnny Black walked up the block,

Sonny Redz said to me, "Dontaye, I've watched you for many years. Your momma taught you well out here, but you need to step your game up in the pimpin' business. Get yourself a stable of young, beautiful females hoes, and you'll make some real money."

Johnny Black just nodded his head in agreement.

"Someday I'll recruit some real hoes and move up in pimpin' the game," I responded.

That was the day things had to change. I was on the come up. About five minutes later, I saw a fine-ass youngin' walking down the block. She stood about 5'9" and weighed about 155 pounds with a 38-24-36 frame. She had a light brown complexion and hazel-green eyes. She also had two blonde ponytails, one on each side of her head.

"Oh my God," I said softly. Swiftly, I stepped straight to her and started a conversation. "Hey, beautiful, can I talk to you for a minute? I see you looking all fine and stuff. What's your name?" I asked, while walking up to her.

"My name is Lil' Porsche. You haven't heard of me yet? I'm the greatest and most well-known female rapper out of Washington, D.C.," she replied as we walked down the block.

Lil' Porsche started spitting some of her lyrics, and the more she rapped the more I became mesmerized. Her rap style seemed to be a cross between Lil' Kim and Foxy Brown. Her shit was gangsta. Lil' Porsche and I decided to exchange telephone numbers to keep in contact. She also invited me to her next show, which was later that night at Club 24. I told Lil' Porsche that I'd see her later. Then I gave her a hug and a kiss on the cheek and headed to the Honeycomb Hideout. It was approaching 8:30 p.m., and I needed to check in with Rabbit and Creamy to see if they needed me to handle anything before I left to see Lil' Porsche perform.

When I got home, Rabbit was yelling at Creamy because the money he made was short, and Rabbit had a big problem with that. The one thing a hoe can never get away with is short money. Whether you pimp women or men, the number one rule is never let your hoe bring you short money. Make them live up to a certain potential. If the goal is to make one thousand dollars a night, make the hoe get that money. No exceptions!

Rabbit started beating Creamy's ass, and I kindly stepped off because Momma didn't take no shit. She's about business.

I called a cab about 11:30 p.m., and ten minutes later, I heard the sound of a horn in front of the house. As I darted out the house, I heard a loud boom as if Rabbit slammed Creamy's head through a wall or something. Right after the loud sound, I heard Momma yell, "Bitch, don't ever bring me short money! I'll kill your mutherfuckin' ass! You hear me, bitch? You hear me!"

At midnight, I was walking in the front door of Club 24. Lil' Porsche had my name on the guest list, and I was escorted backstage by two big, muscular security guards.

"Dontaye! Hey, Dontaye! Over here!" Lil' Porsche screamed as I walked backstage.

"What's going on, baby? I told you that I would be here. My word is my bond," I told her, while walking up to her and giving her a big hug.

I couldn't help but notice Lil' Porsche's wardrobe. She had on a pair of black leather thongs, some knee-high black leather stripper boots, and a black star-shaped sticker covering each of her nipples. Her pretty, phat ass protruded from the back of her thongs and the front view of her displayed two of the biggest breasts a man could wish for.

The next thing I knew, it was time for Lil' Porsche to hit the stage. There must have been more than forty dudes in her entourage, and I was right with them. All you could hear was the fans yelling out her lyrics as the music of her hottest song started playing. It must have been two thousand fans, both men and women, holding their drinks, waving their hands in the air, and dancing as Lil' Porsche stood front center on the stage and rocked from side to side to the music.

"A backrub…I show my woman real love. Like a freak in the sheets, I eat my woman's pussy so deep. Deep inside wit' da extra long tongue, baby. I will make you cum, momma, like always. Bustin' your load by the time I suck the second hole, and together. I know how my baby rolls. 'Cuz I buy my bitch real furs, motherfuckers…platinum, gold, diamonds, and all that fine shit, and I ain't gotta go through the drama. 'Cuz what? I'm a real bitch, a drug dealin' bitch, a killa bitch. I stack my paper and all that real shit."

As the crowd jumped around all night, Lil' Porsche continued to rock the microphone. Even after two hours of Lil' Porsche holding the stage down, the fans wanted her to keep going, but the owner had to pull the plug so the other rapper could come on stage. However, when the other rapper stepped on stage, the crowd started booing.

Hours had passed, and it was time to get back to the Honeycomb Hideout. Lil' Porsche gave me a hug before the club's security escorted her to a limousine.

I walked in the house about 2:35 a.m., and after taking a quick shower, I laid in my bed to call it a night. Suddenly, my thoughts began to come together. I jumped up and quickly my plans went straight into effect. I thought about Lil' Porsche and what I had just witnessed, and in my mind, I could see Sonny Redz' face as he told me to step up my pimpin' game and get some hoes that will make some real cash for me. That was the best advice he could have ever given me. I saw so many young females in the club that had much potential, and from that night on, I decided to promote myself as Big D Entertainment.

The next morning, I went to a printing company and had one thousand business cards printed up with the name of my company and my cell phone number. To make it look official, I even had them add a small headshot of me on the left-hand side of the business card.

As I sat having a bite to eat at Twelve Restaurant and Lounge, located at 12th and H Streets in northeast D.C., I realized I had to start juggling my time, insofar as pimpin' my father Creamy and working these new females that I began to pull up on. I also had to have a talk with Rabbit about my new plans and see what would be the best way to pull this shit off.

Shortly after I left Twelve Restaurant and Lounge, I caught a cab home, or should I say to the Honeycomb Hideout. When I went to put my key in the door, I realized it was unlocked and slightly ajar, which was very unusual. I slowly entered to see if a burglar had intruded our household. As I walked in and tip-toed around, it was so quiet that you could hear a cotton ball drop. Suddenly, I heard a loud scream like someone was in pain. The voice was sort of deep, and all you could hear was, "Oh shit! Oh shit! Oh shit!" Then I heard the person make sounds similar to someone panting while having a baby. The sounds were coming from my mother's bedroom. I ran to my mother's bedroom door and tried to open it, but it was locked.

When I tried turning the doorknob, I heard Rabbit scream, "Who in the fuck is trying to open my mutherfuckin' door? Who the fuck is that?"

"It's Dontaye, Momma. Is everything okay?" I asked with much curiosity.

"Yeah, baby, I'm okay. I'm taking care of a personal client in here."

Momma would never allow me to meet or see any of her personal clients. She always told me that smart people keep their business to themselves. Never let anyone know your secrets or who the major players are in your circle. She always told me that most women have a man or two in their life that their husband or boyfriend didn't know about. The secret male friend to the woman knows everything about her, but she knows nothing about him.

"When most of them bitches get married, as wives, they have three men: a husband, a friend, and a lover," she told me. On the flip side of that, she also said, "A man should keep three women: a wife, a girlfriend, and a hoe. Just make sure each of them have their own money, a car, and a wonderful place to stay. Never fuck with a broke bitch, because they only plot on you and cause drama."

All of those thoughts ran through my mind as I stood at her

door, but suddenly, I looked at my watch and walked away. Noticing it was 4:30 p.m., I had forgotten that Momma had three clients that she saw three times a week on a regular basis between the hours of 1:00 p.m. and 5:30 p.m. So, I decided I would go in my room and watch some television.

I turned to the Channel 5 evening news just as they were reporting on three area men who had robbed a bank with high-powered rifles and AK-47 machine guns. That shit was gangsta! The dudes were not faking, and they meant business. As the news crew and the interviewer were on the scene to interview a store owner, they captured footage of the robbery in progress and the shootout between the robbers and the D.C. Metropolitan Police.

As I watched the news, I noticed a former classmate of mine named Rick and his twin brother Rock in the shootout. Rick and Rock both had an AK-47, while the other person had a rifle. As the three of them ran with big bags of money in one hand and the high-powered weapons in the other, the twins carjacked a woman for her gray 2008 Ford Mustang. Just as they drove off, the third person dove into the window of the Mustang. Several police cars began to chase the stolen Mustang. Suddenly, shots were fired, and you could hear tires screeching during the chase.

Channel 5 posted a special report and had their helicopter following them from the sky. From the news footage Channel 5 showed during the chase, I could see Rock pointing the AK-47 at the helicopter and firing many shots at them as the car sped through the busy traffic of New York Avenue in northeast D.C. The car continued through Ivy City onto Mount Olive Road in Trinidad in front of the 24-hour store. When the car finally came to a stop, all three of them jumped out and ran through an alley and past the side of the store onto Simms Place, and then went their separate ways. The metropolitan police and FBI officials searched the entire Trinidad area for seven days but didn't find a trace of them.

Three days into the beginning of the new week, Rabbit and I finally got a chance to discuss my plan. When I told Rabbit about the new hoes I planned to pimp, she told me just what she thought.

"First and foremost, you need to incorporate a lot of swagger in your pimp game. Then you need to be able to live up to that image. You must be fresh, clean-cut, and always well-dressed from head to toe. Your vocabulary has to be up to par, and you must be able to think quickly in every situation. In this game, you got to make a bitch understand that it's all about you," she said as she took a long puff of her cigarette.

"Your top bitch is the one you treat like a wife. Your second and third in line, you treat them like your pet, and those nothing bitches, you treat them like shit. You keep your foot in their ass until they get that money right," Rabbit added while pouring some Remy Martin VSOP in a tall glass.

Being that Momma had to lay low and stay away from the track, I had to create this empire and run it better than any man that ever played the game. My cell phone rang as I took my shirt off. It was Lil' Porsche.

"Hey, stranger. What's up with you?" I asked as I started running my bathwater.

"Man, I'm bored as hell!" she said, sounding frustrated.

"Well, let's meet up about 5:30 or so and do something, baby," I replied.

"Like what?" she asked.

"Let's go shopping. I have a few hundred in my pocket. I'm sure you will see something you like," I responded, while sitting in a bathtub of warm water and bubbles.

We decided to meet at Martini's on 12th and H Streets Northeast. It was early in the afternoon, so I decided I'd take a nap until 3:30 p.m. just to make sure I was full of energy when I met up with her.

Hours had passed, and I got to Martini's about 5:15 p.m. shortly after Lil' Porsche pulled up in a 2006 candy-apple red Mercedes Benz. She got out and ran up to me as fast as she could. I hugged her tightly as I kissed her forehead.

"What's up, Ms. Porsche, the greatest rapper in the nation's capital?"

"Nothing much. I just need to do something different. You know what I mean? I do the same shit every day. If I ain't writing, I'm in the studio," she said, looking around.

We jumped in the Benz and went to Tyson's Corner Mall in Virginia, where I bought a pair of black Chanel 8-inch stilettos for her. They were black with a white letter C on the right side of the shoe.

"Thank you, Dontaye. I love these shoes so much. I really do," Lil' Porsche said with a huge smile.

"No problem, baby. I would do this all year if I could," I told her as we got in the red Mercedes Benz.

During our ride back to the District of Columbia, Lil' Porsche began talking about her family. She told me how she ran away from home at a very early age and never returned. Some of the things she told me, I couldn't believe what I was hearing.

"When I was four years old, my mother put me and my baby brother in the backseat of a stolen car in seatbelts and drove it into the Potomac River. She jumped out as it began to sink in the river. She didn't know my father had taught me how to swim when I was three, but unfortunately, my baby brother died. He was only two months old," Lil' Porsche said as tears rolled down her face.

"Why did she do that?" I asked with an inquisitive tone.

"Her new boyfriend didn't want kids, so she decided to do what she had to do to be with him."

"Wow!" I could not believe what I was hearing.

She went on to tell me how she was sexually abused by a female babysitter at the age of ten. That went on until she reached her early teens. Lil' Porsche explained to me that she never had sex with a man and had no desire to.

"I'm twenty-seven years old, and not one time have I ever had a real dick in my mouth or pussy. I couldn't tell you how hot cum from a penis feels like," she said as pulled herself together and wiped the tears from her face.

Damn, I knew it was something about her, but I couldn't put my finger on it. I thought to myself as we continued down the highway. Thoughts began to jump around in my head as I daydreamed about having sex with Lil' Porsche. It's every man's dream to have sex with a lesbian woman, especially the ones who have never had a dick before. Deciding to get in her head for a moment, I thought I'd ask her a few questions.

"Lil' Porsche, if you never had sex with a man, how do you know you wouldn't like it?" I asked with curiosity.

"I never said I wouldn't like it. I said I don't desire to find out what it would feel like," Lil' Porsche replied firmly.

"Are you in a relationship with anyone at the moment?" I

inquired.

"Hell yeah!" she yelled with conviction.

"How do you satisfy her sexually?"

She laughed and said, "With soft music and making the bed rock all night long."

Even though I wanted to hear the explicit things they did in the bed, I guess she figured she had said enough for me to use my imagination.

As we crossed over into the District of Columbia, Lil' Porsche told me that she was an exotic dancer, as well. She told me that she danced at three locations where gay women came out to support a dominate and feminine entertainment company.

"I dance for an entertainment company called Secret Admire Entertainment. We perform at the Aqua Nightclub on New York Avenue in northeast D.C., the DeLa Swan Club on Ardwick Ardmore Road, and the Delta Club," she informed me with enthusiasm.

On Thursday night, Lil' Porsche took me to the Aqua Nightclub where she performs as an exotic dancer. The crowd called out her name loudly as she made her way to the stage. I could not believe what I was seeing. Many of her fans that had come to see her rap were many of the same fans that came to see her dance.

"Porsche! Porsche! Porsche!" the crowd screamed as she

danced her way to the stage.

Lil' Porsche came out with a tight black leather outfit on with the Chanel stilettos I bought her. DJ Betty-B played "Between Me and You" by JaRule as Lil' Porsche started shaking her nice, fine ass across the stage. About one hundred and fifty women ran up to the stage and started throwing large bundles of cash at her, mainly one dollar bills.

As Lil' Porsche pulled her leather suit down to her ankles, she kicked her stilettos off. After snatching off the outfit, she dropped down to the floor in a split, rolled over, jumped up, and ran over to a beautiful female that was sitting in a chair. Unexpectedly, Lil' Porsche flipped into her lap upside down, lining up her pussy with the young lady's face.

It seemed as if the whole club went bananas. The women started giving each other high-fives and throwing more money on Lil' Porsche as she gave the woman a hardcore lap dance. The woman in the chair pulled money from every pocket; she had to reward Lil' Porsche for her performance. Suddenly, the crowd started going wild when the song "Big Momma Thang" by Lil' Kim started playing. More women went over to Lil' Porsche and threw piles of one dollar bills all over her as she pulled a chair up to the center of the stage and got Nikki Cash to sit in it.

Nikki Cash was another dancer that danced for Secret

Admire Entertainment. A native of Brazil, she was known for her pretty face and gorgeous measurements of 36-24-36. Rumor had it Nikki Cash was so horny one night, she put four strawberries in her pussy and one banana in her asshole as she danced over to a beautiful Latin female, who slowly ate the fruit from her pussy and ass. Nikki Cash was one horny bitch.

As Lil' Porsche danced to Lil' Kim, she began to get extremely freaky. She started rubbing her pussy and lick her fingertips while humping the floor and pinching the nipples of her nicely-shaped breast. Lil' Porsche played with her pussy for about ten minutes as she continued humping the floor. Minutes later, she squirted out a large stream of her juices. I had never seen a woman cum that hard. It gushed out as if she had pissed all over the floor.

As DJ Betty-B put on another record, Lil' Porsche vanished into the crowd. After a few drinks of Grey Goose vodka on the rocks, I made my way to the restroom, which was unisex. The minute I walked into the next to the last stall, I heard a lot of moaning. I could hear a female making noise like she was taking nine inches of dick or something. I stepped up on a urinal and looked down into the next stall to see Lil' Porsche bent over the toilet seat holding both of her ass cheeks wide open while a sexy brown-skinned female with shoulder-length hair sucked and licked her asshole. I mean that female was good. She sucked and licked Lil' Porsche's asshole until she fell the fuck out. I was so quiet that neither of them noticed I had been watching them the whole time.

Quickly, the beautiful young woman stood up, opened her tight jeans, and whipped out a thick, long, brown dildo from her pants. She spit in Lil' Porsche's ass crack and then thrust that hard plastic dildo straight in her pussy. The woman fucked Lil' Porsche for about twenty minutes.

Lil' Porsche seemed to have gotten dizzy and fell due to all the action, because she busted her lip on the metal flush handle. The young lady helped Lil' Porsche clean herself up by wiping the blood from her lips with a napkin.

A few females walked in and out of the restroom while all of the action was taking place, but no one bothered them or me for that matter. It was like they didn't see or hear anything. In the meantime, I got down from the urinal. My legs were pretty weak from all the balancing I had been doing on the urinal, but I definitely got an eye full and a much better understanding of why females love to fuck each other.

Chapter 2
THE MONEY MAKER

Every chance I got, I handed out flyers and my business cards. Big D Entertainment was on the come up. For nearly two years, I would add all sorts of women to my stable. I would see many beautiful women leaving the latest hot spots in D.C., and in order to move to the next level in my plans, I was right there to capitalize on each of them.

Since I met so many women in my travels through the city, I decided that I would run an all-lesbian prostitution ring and escort service. I started out with eleven sweet, loyal, money-getting women, and they were all lesbians. They wouldn't take a dick if you paid them with all the money the U.S. Treasury Department could make. I had six feminine and five dominate women, and they all were damn good in bed.

I was cool with an old Korean guy named Mr. Lee, who owned five massage parlors throughout the Washington metropolitan area. He had a lot of clientele across the city, but my prostitution ring and escort service brought new meaning to selling sex. This was something the city had never seen before. As a matter of fact, this was something the whole country had never seen or heard of before. From the day I came into this world, my situation was different. So, being different was not a problem for me at all.

On several occasions, I had gone to Mr. Lee about renting one of his many massage parlors, and each time he would say, "One day. One day, Dontaye. I have to get back to you." I never understood why he'd leave me hanging like that, but deep down inside, I knew one day he'd let me have my way.

On June 1st, three days after talking with Mr. Lee, I got a call from him at 6:15 a.m. that Saturday. He told me to come see him at twelve noon sharp or the deal he had for me would be off. Later that day, I met up with him like he asked, and sure enough, he had some keys so me and the girls could go look at one of the buildings where he once ran his massage parlor.

I called the girls and told them to meet me at the address he wrote down on a small sheet of paper. About an hour later, we all met up at the new spot. We couldn't believe our eyes. It was a great place to make real cash flow. There were six private showers and ten rooms with queen size beds. Each room had a Jacuzzi, bathroom, and a massage table for the guests to get a rubdown. There was a booth with a desk that sat behind what looked like bulletproof glass. Beneath the floor at the desk was an old safe that looked like it had not been used in years. Surveillance cameras with audio were installed in all the rooms and outside the building in order to see and hear everything moving and fucking.

Later the next day, all of the dominate females (doms) went with me to buy sex toys that included: dildos, vibrators, swings, butt plugs, tropical-flavored lubricant, sex instruments of all kinds to please our anticipating customers, and of course, condoms.

Ghetto Storm, Fantasy, Fame, Nia Luv, Rainbow, and myself all packed into the Chance Mobile, my rusty, sky blue 1972 Pinto that I bought from the Central Avenue Auto Auction just days before since I had hit the Maryland lottery for five thousand dollars. I took seventy-five dollars of my winnings and bought the Chance Mobile. I also purchased myself two thousand dollars' worth of clothes, because Momma told me to always dress as if I were the owner of a Fortune 500 company. She'd say, "Look like you belong there, even if you don't!"

About thirty minutes later, we pulled up in front of the sex and pleasure store in Georgetown called, The Freaky Freak. As we entered the store, I saw a young, beautiful, white woman that had the potential to be a good friend to me when I needed one. I let the girls find the things we needed for the massage parlor, while I went to spit some game at the woman that I had set my eyes on.

"Hello, gorgeous. How are you doing?" I asked, walking up to her.

"I'm fine. How may I help you today?" she said, giving me a warm smile.

"Well, I'm here for two reasons. First and foremost, I want to introduce myself. I'm Dontaye, and I find you to be so beautiful that I'd like to be the greatest friend you've ever had, and second, my friends and I would like to purchase every freaky thing you have to please a woman in more ways than one."

She smiled, then laughed for a moment. I guess she was taken by surprise. "Okay, I'm Sandy, the owner of The Freaky Freak. I have many things here to please everyone that enjoys sex," she stated, while bending over to pick up a 12-inch strap-on dildo to show the girls and me.

Sandy walked us through the entire store, showing us every little thing she sold that would please a woman in every way. I started picking up the main things we needed, such as several 12-inch strap-on dildos, KY Jelly, dental dam, black leather whips, butt plugs, sex swings, Ben Wa balls for those that like anal pleasure, choker chains, and many other sexual aides for my clients to reach orgasms like they never have before.

Once we left there, we went to Linen and Things for the things needed to decorate the place. It took us days to get the spot to the way we wanted it.

Later that next week, I got five thousand flyers printed up to promote Big D's Massage Parlor and the sexiest doms and fems in the DMV that worked there. The girls and I went to every hot spot in D.C., Maryland, and Virginia. I mean, we hit the main clubs extremely hard. The next day, calls started pouring in. So many people rang my cell phone that I almost couldn't keep up with the high volume of calls that came in. One woman asked, "Just how private is the location?" Another woman asked, "Can I have three doms massage my body at one time?"

After a brief meeting with the girls on July 4, 2004, we opened for business. Most of our clientele were females from the local gay and lesbian nightclubs. Most of the women would go to the DeLa Swan Club or the Delta Club, which was run by MC Dom Diva, and see the women from Secret Admire Entertainment perform. When the show ended, many of the females would call and make appointments during the night to satisfy their every sexual need.

Our first client was Sugar Momma, one of the most

notorious female drug kingpins in Washington, D.C. Sugar Momma was twenty-four years old, brown-skinned, and had long black hair that reached her mid back. Her shape was out of this world. She stood at 5'9" and had measurements of 33-22-34. One thing about Sugar Momma is she was one tough bitch. She would have your ass killed at the drop of a hat. That's no bullshit!

I had all the girls lined up and seated in the waiting area of the massage parlor where the clients could pick and choose who they wanted to have sex with. When Sugar Momma entered the parlor, she walked directly over to Wet Wet, one of the fems.

"You are the one for me, baby. I don't have to look no further," Sugar Momma said, then placed three thousand dollars on the counter. "Is this enough for her time?"

After counting the money twice, I replied, "Oh yeah, this will get you very good treatment."

As they headed to the first unoccupied room, Sugar Momma turned around and said, "Oh, by the way, I'm Sugar Momma, and you'll be seeing me coming to this spot a lot more."

I looked at her and responded, "I'm glad to have you."

Little did she know, I had already heard so much about her and the drug gang that she led.

When Sugar Momma and Wet Wet entered the room, they removed their clothes and got in the Jacuzzi. As I focused the camera in the room to view them up close, I could see as they started to wash each other. Sugar Momma started sucking on Wet Wet's left nipple, and Wet Wet looked as if she was enjoying the pleasurable feeling of Sugar Momma's touch as she continued to lick and suck her young, beautiful, firm breast.

After washing and a little foreplay, they slowly moved to the massage table. Wet Wet held Sugar Momma's hand and motioned for her to lay face down. As Sugar Momma assumed the position, Wet Wet poured some scented oil onto Sugar Momma's back and down to her butt. She then started massaging Sugar Momma's shoulders and arms slowly for about ten minutes. Next, her hands gave special attention to Sugar Momma's back, rubbing slowly down to her butt cheeks and legs. Wet Wet massaged Sugar Momma scrupulously for about thirty minutes before Sugar Momma turned over so that Wet Wet could eat her throbbing, moist pussy.

"That's right, you young, pretty bitch. Eat my pussy. Eat it, baby. Eat that cum out this muthafucka," Sugar Momma cried out loudly.

Wet Wet's tongue went in and out, and up and down Sugar Momma's pussy for twenty-five minutes. Then it was time to change positions. Sugar Momma got up and told Wet Wet to lay face down on the table. After Wet Wet did as she was told, Sugar Momma started licking her asshole while fingerfucking her hot little pussy with the two middle fingers of her right hand. After a few minutes of sticking her tongue in and out of Wet Wet's ass, Sugar Momma told Wet Wet to turn over on her back. Then she began to lick and suck on Wet Wet's elongated erectile organ located at the anterior part of her vulva. Twenty minutes later, Wet Wet's body began to tremble as little beads of sweat formed on her forehead.

"Damn, you eat pussy so good. I never thought someone could make my pussy feel so good," Wet Wet uttered softly.

Sugar Momma went over to the table covered with sex toys, picked up a 12-inch strap-on dildo, and began strapping it on.

"Get on the bed, sweetheart. I want to fuck that pussy real good, baby," Sugar Momma whispered in Wet Wet's ear.

"I need a good fucking, honey. My pussy is so wet that I can't wait to get something long and stiff up in it," Wet Wet replied, while rubbing on her hot, juicy pussy.

Wet Wet laid back on the bed as Sugar Momma got on top of her.

"Oh baby, that dick is hard going up in my pussy. Shit! Damn, that's a fat, hard dick! I'm gonna take it all! Get this pussy!" Wet Wet yelled as Sugar Momma continued to slide the hard dildo in her tight pussy.

The action started to pick up as they both began to grind harder and harder.

"Oh my goodness! Oh my goodness! Oh...oh...oh...oh shit! Oh...oh shit! I'm cumming! I'm cumming!" Wet Wet screamed as Sugar Momma thrust the dildo all the way inside her.

Wet Wet's body trembled with every stroke, and her juicy pussy had the entire bed soaked from the large load of cum she released. We didn't call her Wet Wet for nothing. Would you like some of her?

Chapter 3
AN IMPORTANT MESSAGE

I received a call from Rabbit at about four-thirty on a Monday morning. I knew something was wrong because I could hear it in her voice.

As I held the telephone receiver to my ear, Momma said, "Your father has just been shot three times, and it don't look like he's gonna make it."

"Momma, what are you talking about?" I asked, not wanting to believe I had heard her right.

"Your father had a date tonight, and the dude didn't know he was transgender. The guy pulled out a .38 special and shot Creamy in the chest, arm, and leg," Momma explained as I heard the ambulance sirens in the background.

"Where are you and Dad now?"

"We're pulling up at Washington Hospital Center. The doctors are rushing out here to get him now."

"I'm on my way, Momma. I'll be there as soon as I can. Don't worry," I told her.

I informed the girls about what had happened and put Ghetto Storm on point, telling her to hold everything down until I got back from the hospital. She told me to go handle my business and that everything would be ran like it would normally. I trusted her a lot and knew she could handle the girls.

After quickly jumping into the Chance Mobile, I headed straight to the hospital. A couple turns here and there, and I was on Florida Avenue. Before I knew it, I hit North Capital Street, took it all the way out to Michigan Avenue, made the left, and then, I was walking into the emergency room.

They operated on Creamy for six hours. The time while we waited gave me the chance to have a long talk with Rabbit about her working for me at the massage parlor. See, Momma was the only person that I would trust in this situation because she taught me the game, just from a different angle. However, I don't know if she would cause problems with the girls and me since she's a lesbian and a player on top of it. I never make excuses for people, whether they're blood or not. When you know someone and know them well, then you know what you're up against. In this case, I had to remember that the girls might cause a bit of temptation when it comes to Momma's weaknesses.

Momma loved to eat pussy and fuck a cunt until it was bone dry. One thing about Rabbit, she would fuck a woman until she couldn't walk. Momma always said, "A man can fuck a woman, but women can fuck a woman much better." I remember several occasions when Momma fucked a few college students so hard that an ambulance had to come to the house and take them to a nearby hospital for surgery. Although Momma would fuck a female into a coma, she truly believed in having a woman experience nothing but great pleasure when it came to sexual intercourse.

As we sat in the waiting room, I gave Momma the spill on the massage parlor, the business, and the girls.

"Momma, I promote my company as Big D Entertainment. I made an illegal business a legal business. As I've told you, I moved on to manage a line of gorgeous women. They're all young and in their mid to late twenties. As well, all of them are lesbian fems and doms."

Momma's eyes got as big as two golf balls when I told her the girls were lesbians. That bit of information made her feel right at home.

"How long have you been in business?" Momma asked, while looking around the emergency room.

"Maybe twenty days, if that long. I know I raked in about fifteen thousand dollars by the second week. I can tell you honestly that this company will make us rich if we run it properly. We will never have to be in the streets again," I expressed with enthusiasm.

As we sat, I told Rabbit everything I needed her to do for my company, and she promised to be down with anything to make this company work. The one thing I know about Momma is she'll die for whatever she commits herself to. She's a true soldier.

After many hours passed, the doctor came out to tell us that Creamy had died from his wounds.

"You mean to tell me that my father has passed away?" I asked with anger, while pacing around the waiting area of the emergency room.

"I'm sorry," the doctor said.

Momma didn't say one word. I believe she was hurt and shocked at the same time.

Moments later, a second doctor rushed out from behind the double doors and yelled out to the doctor we were talking to, saying, "He's alive! The man is alive! We need you back in the operating room."

Without another word, the doctor ran back through the double doors with the other doctor. I couldn't believe my ears when he said my father was alive.

No matter what someone does or who that person is in your family, blood should always be loved. In this day of age, a lot of families are fucked up with no love or loyalty at all. Family members hate on other members. Brothers have become jealous backstabbers to their own brothers. Sisters have become liars and disloyal to their own sisters. Mothers and fathers don't know any moral standards to pass down to their children. That's why the children in the urban neighborhoods are so damn crazy. They haven't been taught any logical morals to live by. I said all that to say, I love my father no matter what or who he is, and I felt he deserved to live just like any other human being.

A few more hours passed before the same doctor returned to tell us that Creamy was alive but in intensive care. He told me and Momma that hopefully in a couple of days he'd be more stable.

Once Rabbit and I left the hospital, I decided to take her to the massage parlor to meet the girls and to see the entire set up. When Rabbit and I arrived, all the girls were in the rooms fucking or sucking some ass, plain and simple. Ghetto Storm had collected the money and kept things running smoothly as I asked her to do.

"What's going on? How have things been going since I've been gone?" I asked as Ghetto Storm handed me a large, brown paper bag filled with cold, hard cash.

"Everything went fine, Dontaye, just as it should have. I really didn't ask what services the customers wanted. I just charged a flat rate for today of three hundred dollars an hour. Was that cool?"

"Yeah, that's cool. I'll let everyone know what the prices are for the different services during our next meeting."

I introduced Rabbit to Ghetto Storm and to each of the girls as they finished servicing the clients.

"I want all my fems to stand beside me so you can meet my mother," I said as everyone piled into the front room of the parlor where the security desk was located. "Ok, Mom, this is the crew. Everyone step up and say your name. Fems first."

As Princess, Doneesha, Kat, Wet Wet, Nikita Sunshine, and Sweet Money Reds stated their names, my mother nodded her head in approval. Next, the doms stepped up to introduce themselves. Once Fantasy, Nia Luv, Fame, Rainbow, and Ghetto Storm introduced themselves, Momma looked impressed. She couldn't do nothing but stand there speechless. She had raised me into a beast. I became a master at the game and was good at what I was taught. I just did something different, something other pimps and players wouldn't be able to pull off.

Since everyone was together, I used the opportunity to talk

to the girls about the things I planned to do as we continued to move up to the next level.

"Every day that goes by needs to be better than yesterday. Our primary goals are MONEY, POWER, LOYALTY, AND SUCCESS. No ifs, ands, or buts about it. If everyone wants to be rich, then you need to stick with me, plain and simple."

The girls all nodded in agreement. They believed in my approach to gain the finer things in life. I could clearly see that I had to give them some reassurance from time to time, something to look forward to, some initiative.

"Okay, everybody, here are some of the prices, and as we know, any and everything goes. One minute to twenty minutes is $300.00. Thirty minutes is $400.00. One hour is $1,000.00, and anything up to three hours is $3,000.00. If anyone wants to know the overnight prices, tell them to speak with me."

Before I could finish, the telephone began to ring constantly. Clients were making appointments like crazy. I even began to notice some new faces. One new face was a female who claimed to be a high-profile criminal attorney that handled one of the largest cocaine kingpin cases in the District of Columbia. I was a little skeptical to have my girls service her at first, but shit, with her being an attorney, I thought I might need her to defend me someday. She warned us to keep a low profile, and if we did, she promised to be a customer forever.

"I'm Lisa Watts, one of the most well-known attorneys in the United States. I won more trials than any trial lawyer in this country. I'm also the most paid legal officer in the court system, too," she said, while turning her hourglass figure around for us all to see.

Lisa Watts chose Rainbow to trick with, and as they headed to Room #2, I looked at the monitor that was hooked up for that particular room. I absolutely had to see how Lisa Watts got her rocks off, and I had a feeling it was going to be one hot fuck session.

Lisa Watts was a black gal. She had on a sky blue business skirt suit with a white blouse. She was fly. Rainbow began taking off Lisa's clothes one piece at a time until she got down to her black thong underwear. I can't describe Lisa's measurements, but if you can envision Ice's T's woman CoCo's body, you'll better understand what she's working with. Now, in the face, she would remind you of Alicia Keys. Lisa Watts was a sho' nuff ten.

After Rainbow took off her sports bra, raggedy jeans, and Timberland boots, she turned on the faucet to the Jacuzzi and poured bubble bath into the water. As the water filled the Jacuzzi, Rainbow and Lisa started holding each other tightly while locking lips. Then Rainbow started sucking on Lisa's breasts, giving special attention to her nipples as she sucked and licked them until they were standing up firm and hard. Lisa began sucking on Rainbow's breasts, as well, until her nipples were just as hard. They continued sucking on each other, until Rainbow took her hand and led her over to the Jacuzzi. Lisa got in first.

"Oh shit, the water is ice cold," Lisa said, as she sat and began to shiver.

"Don't think about it. I'm gonna take care of that. I'm here to warm you up, baby," Rainbow whispered, as she lathered up the washcloth and started to wash Lisa's trembling body.

Rainbow washed Lisa's body for several minutes before she started licking and sucking on her pink clit that protruded from her juicy, clean shaven pussy lips. As Rainbow stuck her tongue in and out of Lisa's pussy, Lisa laid restlessly in the cold bubble bath water with her eyes rolling back in her head.

"Damn, this feels good. Oh my goodness. You'll suck my pussy into a coma," Lisa moaned as she held on to Rainbow's head with both hands.

Rainbow motioned Lisa to sit up on the side of the Jacuzzi with both legs wide open. Then she started sucking on Lisa's pussy aggressively, while sticking her index finger in, out, and around her wet, juicy pussy as she sucked, sucked, sucked on Lisa's thick, pink clitoris.

"I'm cumming! Shit! I'm cumming! Oh my goodness, I'm

cumming!" Lisa screamed as her body shook uncontrollably.

Rainbow pulled Lisa across the floor to the bed, strapped on a 12-inch dildo, and started fucking Lisa right beside the bed.

With her teeth clinched tight, Rainbow uttered, "My dick stays hard all night long," while grinding slowly into Lisa.

Thirty-five minutes had passed, and Rainbow began to pick up speed as she banged Lisa's pussy.

"I'm cumming again! I'm cumming! Oh shit!"

Lisa grabbed Rainbow, rolled on top of her, moved the strap-on dildo to the side, and began licking her slightly hairy pussy. She sucked and licked around the clit of Rainbow's pussy until she began to cum.

Rainbow quickly regrouped because she knew time was money and the room needed to be ready for the next customer. While they began putting on their clothes, Lisa Watts had a look on her face as if she found what she had been looking for. As they say, it's very lonely at the top, and I had a feeling we would be seeing a lot more of Lisa Watts.

Chapter 4
FROM BIGGER TO BETTER

Now that the money was rolling in, I decided to buy myself a real car—something that would turn heads when I drove by or stopped at a red light. So, the first thing I did was go on the internet and look at the CarMax website. I saw many great cars, but I had to have one that fit my needs and personality. I looked at many different types before making up my mind. A silver 2003 SL500 Mercedes Benz caught my eye. It had an automatic transmission, gray leather interior, and got fifteen miles to the gallon in the city and twenty-two mile per gallon on the highway. For the money they wanted for the car, I felt it was a great deal.

I contacted CarMax, told them that I wanted to purchase the car, and the rest was history. As I pulled off the lot with my 2003 SL500 Mercedes Benz, a motherfucker couldn't tell me shit on that day. When I pulled up in front of the massage parlor, the girls were sitting on the porch. Suddenly, when they noticed it was me, they all jumped up and ran to the car.

"Dontaye, I love it! I love the car!" Nikita Sunshine yelled as she ran up to the driver's side door.

Nia Luv, Fame, and Sweet Money Reds jumped into the car and asked me to take them for a ride. So, I drove them from the massage parlor to the Verizon Center, which was on the other side of downtown Washington, D.C.

We stopped and got a bite to eat at Legal Seafood on 7th Street NW. As the girls and I were being seated, we noticed a female sitting next to our table. It looked to me that I had seen this woman before, but I just couldn't figure out where. As people began to crowd around her table, all you could hear was, "Can I get your autograph, Ricey?" One lady even pushed a couple of people out of her way while holding a pad and pen out to the lady.

Suddenly, it hit me like a ton of bricks. "It's the famous golfer, Ricey Labella," I said under my breath.

The first thing I thought about was giving her one of my business cards, because I could remember reading in the *Washington Post* newspaper about her being gay and how she was planning to marry her girlfriend at the time. Several months later, they broke up because Ricey walked into her five-million-dollar mansion and caught the bitch in bed having sex with a woman she had met in a bar the night Ricey won the PGA Championship.

Ricey Labella was a thick white woman with a sexy shape. I had a good chance to speak with Ricey because she was seated right next to the girls and me. When her bodyguards made the large crowd of people leave her table, I used the opportunity to hand her one of my cards.

"Hey, Ricey, I'm Dontaye. How are you?"

"I'm fine now that I can finally get something to eat. I love all my fans and try to always sign autographs for them, but sometimes it can get to be a bit much," Ricey said as she took the business card from my outstretched hand.

"I own Big D's Massage Parlor, and the girls are all lesbians. My doms are very sexy with tight bodies, and my fems are all drop-dead gorgeous. You should come and check us out. The first massage is on the house."

"Okay, Dontaye, I will come. I do need to get away. I'm in need of some TLC. Can I come in a few weeks?" Ricey asked.

"Sure. We'll be waiting to give you our best service, Ricey. Call me when you're on the way to the parlor," I said as the waiter came over to take our orders.

Ricey and I talked for another two hours before we finally said goodbye. I could tell she enjoyed the things we had talked about, especially the massage parlor. When I described what the girls looked like, I could see the lust in her eyes. At that point, I knew I would be seeing her sooner than one would think.

Chapter 5

STICK WITH WHAT YOU KNOW

Over the past few months, the female drug kingpin Sugar Momma and I had been hanging out together. We took trips to Los Angeles, Atlanta, New York City, and we even went to see a boxing match in Las Vegas between Bernard Hopkins and Winky Wright.

"Dontaye, I want you to think about doing some major business with me—I mean, major," Sugar Momma said, putting her hand on my shoulder.

"What kind of business are you talking about?" I asked while looking deep into her cold, murderous eyes. "You know I'm not into selling drugs."

"Well, you won't have to sell anything. We can have the girls sell to your clients, and you can get rich that way, too. Look, I sell about five thousand kilos a week. I sell my kilos for fifteen thousand a pop and make an easy $30,000.00 a month," Sugar Momma said as we began walking to her white on white 2007 S-type Jaguar.

Sugar Momma and I talked for a few hours about our plans in partnership. I really didn't feel comfortable about the idea, but the money sounded good. Even though I was pulling in a whopping fifteen thousand a week, I thought to myself, *A person can never have enough money.*

"Well, I don't know, Sugar Momma. I got to think about this because I don't want to see my clients fucked up. I need them to spend their money with me and have a good time doing it. You feel me?" I said, while getting into the passenger side of her Jaguar.

During the ride back to the massage parlor, Sugar Momma tried to convince me to deal drugs. The shit she was telling me really sounded good, but Rabbit always told me that a wise man always gets better with his craft and to always stick with what you know.

My cell phone rang several times, and as I pushed the green button to answer, I could clearly see it was Lil' Porsche. I hadn't heard from her in a few weeks and was glad to know she was thinking about me.

"Hey, slim. What's up with ya, babe?"

"Nothin' much, Dontaye. I had a show last night at the

Twelve Lounge, and I have another one tonight. Since I haven't seen you in a while, I thought I would call you to see if you can come tonight."

"You damn right I can make it, girl. You're my baby. What time is it gonna start, boo?"

"It's gonna start about eleven o'clock," she told me before we hung up.

I told Sugar Momma about Lil' Porsche and asked if she wanted to go to the club with me. Sugar Momma said she had been hearing about Lil' Porsche. She also said she had seen posters all around the Washington metropolitan area about the shows and the places she performs. I was glad to hear that Lil' Porsche was making a buzz around the city. *Maybe we have a great female rapper in the making,* I thought to myself.

On the way back to the massage parlor, I asked Sugar Momma when did she realize she was gay and why did she become a lesbian. At first, it seemed as if I caught her by surprise with the question. But, then again, it seemed as if she had been waiting to talk to someone for years about her sexual orientation and the loyalty she had for her lifestyle. Usually Sugar Momma spoke with conviction and on a level of total confidence, but her first few words were very soft and mild.

"Wow, I didn't expect you to ask me something like that, but it's a good question. My first boyfriend Bubbles was a well-known drug dealer around D.C. I was so in love with him, and unlike a lot of females who lose respect for men and do all types of sneaky shit, I was loyal. I never cheated. I never gave my number out or gave a man the opportunity to try his hand at getting with me," she expressed while we were stopped at a red light.

Sugar Momma went on to tell me how her ex-boyfriend Bubbles sold millions of dollars' worth of heroin and cocaine throughout the D.C., Maryland, and Virginia areas.

"The things this nigga had is the shit niggas dream of having their entire lifetime. For starters, we lived in a $6.5 million dollar mansion in Hollywood, California, and commuted from home to Washington, D.C. by air on a weekly basis so he could get his drug money and we could see our families for a few hours. We had matching diamond watches, platinum diamond chains and rings, platinum diamond bracelets, fur coats, and all types of expensive cars, like Lamborghini, Ferrari, and the Bentley. The E Class Mercedes Benz was our hooptie. He was famous for saying, 'Life Is Good'. Anyway the shit that broke my heart and flipped me out my fuckin' mind was when I caught this nigga in our bedroom having sex with one of his workers."

"Was Bubbles fucking the dude?" I asked.

"No, the dude was fucking Bubbles. Not to mention the

dude had a very large dick. The dude fucked Bubbles from the back so hard that his platinum chain flew off his neck and clean across the room. The dude was pounding that dick in his ass like a jackhammer going through cement. I just couldn't understand how he took all that dick with no problem," she said in a confused tone.

Sugar Momma went on to tell me how that traumatized her and how she felt she had nothing to live for because he was the only person that meant anything to her at the time. She said she loved him more than she loved herself.

I was stuck and couldn't speak a word because I couldn't imagine her going through something like that. Looking at her from the outside, you would never think a woman like her would experience something that tragic.

"So, after I got over him and that situation, it was very hard for me to let my guard down," Sugar Momma continued. "Months later, I met a guy named Random Rob. He was also a big-time drug dealer. He was not as big as Bubbles in the drug game, but he had a lot of cash. He treated me well, but I caught him in our house having sex with four females. I watched them fuck for hours, and the more I watched, the more I was turned on. That's when I began to understand that I didn't like men anymore," she said with a pleasant smirk on her face.

"It was this fine bitch in the bunch named Yolanda. Later, I found out she was a model. This bitch was so fuckin' pretty, and she had the biggest ass you could ever see. Immediately, I jumped into the group sex session, pulled Yolanda to the floor, and started sucking her pussy. I sucked on Yolanda's pussy for about an hour while sticking my middle finger in and out of her tight pussy hole. The lips on her pussy begin to swell as I continued to suck and swallow all of her sweet juices." Sugar Momma paused to lick her lips with her long, thick tongue, as if she could taste Yolanda at that very moment.

"So what happened next?" I asked.

"Well, I liked Yolanda so much that I started using his money to take her on shopping sprees, wine and dine her, take her on trips, and purchase her expensive gifts. I fell in love with the bitch. Yolanda and I had many sexual experiences together, and I became the nigga to her that many bitches wished they had."

Sugar Momma's story got so good to me that I didn't realize we were back at the massage parlor so fast. I got out the car and told her that I would be ready to go to the show about ten o'clock p.m. She told me that she had a few runs to make first and then she would go home to freshen up. Before she pulled off, I told her that I wanted to hear the rest of her story later. That shit sounded like something out of a book or movie.

Once she drove away, I noticed four men sitting in a car

across the street from the massage parlor. They looked to be undercover cops to me, but I really couldn't see them all that clearly.

Hours later, Sugar Momma pulled up in front of the massage parlor, and we were off to the show at Twelve Lounge. First, though, Sugar Momma stopped at Viggy's Liquor Store on 15th Street NE. When we went inside, Sugar Momma saw a dude that owed her some money. That's when all hell broke loose.

She walked up on the dude and asked him to step outside. As the guy stepped out the door, Sugar Momma pulled out a small .380 handgun and smacked him upside the head a few times. The dude just dropped to his knees and then his whole body fell to the ground. Sugar Momma pointed the pistol at the dude as he lay on the ground, but someone walked out the liquor store behind us. So, she put the small pistol in the waistline of her tight Ecko Unlimited blue jeans, and then we got back in the Jaguar and pulled off.

"Damn, Sugar Momma, you don't be fakin'. You pistol whipped the shit out that dude. That dude's face was leaking blood everywhere," I said as we headed for Twelve Restaurant and Lounge.

"It's not a game when it comes to my money. It's so many people out here that try to be slick and con people out of shit these days. They get your money and don't have any intentions on paying you back. Those kind of people have to be dealt with. I'ma knock a bone off a motherfucker's head," Sugar Momma said, while looking at me with her murder-filled eyes.

When we pulled up in front of Twelve Lounge, there was a large crowd in front of the door and a long line around the block. One thing I knew was when we got in, it was going be on. Twelve Restaurant and Lounge is known for having some of the greatest parties in the Washington, D.C. area. The parties are off the hook.

Sugar Momma and I walked up to the front of the line to where the owner was standing.

"What's up, Sugar Momma? How are you, sweetheart?" the owner said, hugging her briefly.

Sugar Momma didn't crack a smile. She kept it gangsta. When the owner let her go, she started toward the front door and never looked back. When we got inside, it was just as I thought. It was jam-packed and the ladies were looking damn good.

We went straight for the bar and had a few drinks. If you understand the club life, you will get loose after you take a few shots of Grey Goose. We danced and partied like I had never done before. Then I saw this lil' honey sitting at the bar all by herself, so I decided to go at her since I was off the drinks and feeling good. You know how that drink can have you feeling like your rap game is on one hundred.

"Hey, beautiful, how are you tonight?" I asked when I got close up on her.

"I'm fine. How about yourself?" she said, looking at me with a slight freaky gaze.

I could clearly see she could be mine for the taking, so I ran game like real players do. I started up a conversation with her on her beauty and sexiness. I told her that I worked in the entertainment business and was looking for beautiful women like her to be part of my entertainment company for many reasons. I also expressed how I found her to be breathtaking and her beauty much pleasing to the eyes. This bitch was outstanding, and I had to have her all to myself.

"We are steady talking, and I don't know your name," she softly whispered.

"Oh damn, my fault, baby. My name is Dontaye, and yours?" I said, sticking my hand out to shake hers.

"I'm Envy. Pleased to meet you. I'm here with my cousin Juicy. She just broke up with her boyfriend of four years, so we're celebrating. I told her to break up with his bum ass six months into their relationship, but that's a story we don't need to discuss. You're not a bum ass dude are you?"

"No, not at all, sweetheart. I can show you better than I can tell, though. Here, take my card and call me. I think we'll be real good friends. I'm here with a very good friend, and I want to get back over there to chill with her, but you make sure you call me," I told her, then handed the bartender a hundred dollar bill to pay for Envy and Juicy's drinks for the night.

"Hey, wait for a moment, Dontaye. Here's my card, too. I work at Greater Southeast Hospital. My cell phone number is on there, also. Call me, baby," Envy said as she blew a kiss at me and winked her right eye.

Even though I had a stable of lesbian escorts and a rap game that could pull almost any woman, I felt a serious connection with Envy from the very start. I felt there was something more to her than what the eye could see. I wanted to have this woman in a way that she had never been had before.

Envy stood about 5-feet, 9-inches and weighed about 155 pounds. She was light brown skin with long black hair down to her shoulders. Her ass was as phat as Jennifer Lopez or even Kim Kardashian. *She has one ass I got to fuck!*

After leaving Envy, I made my way back over to Sugar Momma. The crowded club got extremely live when the deejay played a song off the Biggie Smalls album *Mo Money, Mo Problems.*

Even though Sugar Momma was gangsta and had a killer-type attitude, she did have a soft side, also. We danced for a while, and even though she had a nice phat ass, the thought never crossed my mind to put my fat dick on her ass. If you've ever seen the movie *Get Rich or Die Tryin'* by 50 Cent, Sugar Momma looked just like the woman that played his mother.

A few hours had passed, and we were ready to leave. Before doing so, I sent more drinks over to Envy and Juicy so they could enjoy themselves. I did get to share one dance with Envy before Sugar Momma and I left, and it was hot. When I got on Envy's ass, my dick blew up like a quarter-pounder beef hot dog—the kind you buy from the 7-11 convenience stores. Feeling the dick in the crack of her ass, she grabbed it with her right hand to measure its length and width. Then she turned and looked at me like she approved of the size.

Envy gave me a kiss on the cheek and said, "I can't wait to put it in my ass."

Shocked but pleased with her forwardness, I looked at her and replied, "I'm gonna lick that hole like it's never been licked before. Then I'm gonna stuff it like I'm stuffing a turkey on Thanksgiving Day, babes. I got you."

She licked her lips, grabbed her breast, and responded, "Give me the best you got. That's all I ask."

Her words caused butterflies in my chest. You know the kind you get when you're nervous? Yeah, that's the kind I'm talking about. I stepped off at that point.

I saw Sugar Momma heading toward the door, but just as we reached the doorway to leave the club, I heard an angry woman yell out, "Yeah, bitch, we meet again! How you wanna carry it now?"

Sugar Momma and I both stopped in our tracks. As we turned around to follow the sound of the angry voice, a woman ran up on Sugar Momma, and they started wrecking on the spot. The bitch that ran up on Sugar Momma was one fine-ass bitch that looked just like the singer Ashanti. The two females fought like to men. If I had to describe the fight, I would say it was the match between Mike Tyson and Evander Holyfield. They stayed close up on each other, going toe to toe with nonstop swinging. They threw punches at each other for about twenty minutes. It was a fight that should've earned one of them a WBA World Championship title.

The police started through the crowd of people, but by the time they got to the spot where it had taken place, Sugar Momma and the other bitch were gone. We finally made it back to the car. Sugar Momma's nose was bleeding and her face was starting to swell in certain places.

"Sugar Momma, who in the hell was that woman you were fighting?" I asked with concern.

"Oh, that was some bitch named Solo. We use to be partners at one time, until someone stole one hundred kilos of cocaine from one of our stash spots. I believe she stole the cocaine, and she believes I killed her mom. This beef will never die, at least not until one of us is dead. There that bitch go right there!" Sugar Momma said, then jumped out of the car and took off running to the corner of 11th and H Streets NE.

Pulling out her .380 caliber pistol, she shot at Solo several times before running back to the Jaguar and pulling off at high speed.

"This shit is going to come to a head at some point. Either I'm going to kill this hoe or the bitch is gonna kill me. It can't keep going down like this, trust me."

As we drove down Florida Avenue toward New York Avenue, a red 500 Mercedes Benz pulled up beside us. The tinted window on the passenger side slowly lowered, and all I could see was a person with sunglasses on and a black hoodie over their head pointing a .9mm semi-automatic hand pistol at us. Suddenly, shots were fired at us, and all the windows were shot out except for the front window.

Sugar Momma pulled off at high speed, and the Mercedes pulled off right with us. However, the Benz made a quick right onto New York Avenue, while we kept straight on Florida Avenue.

"Are you okay, Dontaye?" Sugar Momma asked as she shook my trembling body.

"Oh shit! Yeah, I'm okay. I'm cool," I replied, while looking around at the shattered windows.

I must admit those were two go hard bitches, and I had a feeling the shit wasn't going to get no better.

We never got the chance to see Lil' Porsche perform that night, but I'm very sure she rocked the stage like she always did.

Chapter 6
LICKY LICKY

It was on a Saturday night. I'd never forget. I was sitting in the massage parlor with the girls, and the telephone rang. It had to have been about 11:30 p.m. It was so busy that night I picked the telephone up on the very last ring. I knew it was the last ring because the answering service will pick up the call after the tenth ring.

Anyway, a customer asked to speak with one of the girls. I found that to be unusual since the girls were not allowed to talk to anyone under any conditions, unless I told them to do so.

"Excuse me. May I talk to one of the young ladies that works there?" the caller asked.

I tried to figure out if it was a joke of some sort, because no one had ever just called with such a request. I was blown and didn't know if it was the police doing an investigation or someone trying to get in my business. So, I told the person that they had the wrong number and hung up. About twenty minutes later, the phone rang again. I answered, and it was the same voice.

"May I speak to one of the ladies that works there, please?" the low, soft-toned voice pleaded.

"May I ask who this is, please?" I asked.

"This is a friend of MC Dom Diva. I got this number from someone at the club that you gave your card to some time ago."

"What's your name?" I asked the woman.

"Money," the woman replied slowly.

The first thing I said in my mind was that she had the right name, because money is what I hunted for on a daily basis.

When I asked Money how I could help her, she said, "You can start by giving me the address so I can come through and pay you to have someone there make me cum. I like women, so I'm already on point as to what your program is all about. All I want to do is lick a nice pretty ass until I cum a few times. That's all I want to do."

After providing Money with the address, forty minutes later she was at the front door. I buzzed her in, and from the look on her face, I could tell she was ready for some serious action.

I extended my hand out to her and said, "Hey there. I'm

Dontaye."

She shook my hand and replied, "And I'm Money."

Money was a fine young lady. She looked to be about twenty-one or twenty-two years old. She stood about five foot even and looked to weigh about 130 pounds. She also had a beautiful brown skin complexion. She was so beautiful that I wouldn't have ever thought she had a lesbian bone in her.

Anyway, she explained to me that she had an ass fetish and an obsession for licking clean assholes that smelled like soap.

"I like big asses, and I love sucking pussy, too, but a woman's asshole is just so attractive to me. I can cum at just the thought of sucking an ass."

Hearing her cry, I called out one of my fems, Nikita Sunshine, who was one fine-ass bitch. If Money wanted to go out with the biggest sexual bang of her life, then Nikita would be the one she would never forget.

The two went into Room #3, and as you know, I had to have the cameras on for the protection of the girls at all times. Money had on a short blue dress, but as she as got in the room, she pulled the dress over her head and started to pull Nikita Sunshine's short skirt down, too. Wasting no time, Money started licking the crack of her ass. All I could see was Money's tongue going in and out of Nikita's ass as I used the camera to zoom in on the action.

It seemed to me that Nikita was enjoying every bit of the ass licking. Actually, Nikita went and got some wild cherry syrup to add flavor to the ass-licking experience for Money. As Money sucked Nikita's ass, she played with her own shaved pussy. You could see her clit sticking straight out as if she wanted it licked and sucked, too. She even stuck her middle finger in her own asshole as she continued licking and sucking Nikita Sunshine's ass.

"Oh my...oh my! Damn! Shit! Right there, boo! Right there!" Money screamed.

Suddenly, all I could see was her pussy juice squirting all over the floor. When she finally came, she seemed to be exhausted, but she sure did look satisfied. After Money put her dress on, she hugged Nikita tightly and then smacked her ass before walking out of the room.

Although Money paid a good piece of change in the beginning, she still left a nice tip for Nikita. Money said she'd be back soon, and I told her that she was welcome to come back anytime.

Chapter 7
MMMM GOOD

Several days after I met Envy, I got a telephone call from her on a Friday morning. The telephone rang about five times before I finally answered.

"Good morning. Are you up yet?"

"Who's this?" I asked.

"This is Envy, babes. If you want me to call you back, I'll do that."

"No. Everything's cool. What's up?" I asked, while rubbing the sleep out of my eyes.

"I was thinking about you, and I want you to come to my job this morning so I can suck your dick in my office. Can you make it before my boss comes in?" Envy asked with a seductive tone.

"Where, over to Greater Southeast Hospital?"

"Yeah, I work in communications. Just come in the middle building and walk past the security officer's desk. I'll see you. I'm right beside the elevators. Hurry up. I want to suck your dick, and I also want you to fuck me in the ass, boo."

Before hanging up, Envy explained to me how bad she wanted to get fucked in her mouth and up her rectum. She said that if I was going to be her man, it was a must that I fuck her up the ass at least four times a week, not to mention her fat, juicy pussy.

Immediately, I washed up, jumped in my Benz, and headed her way. Before I knew it, I was at the hospital and walking through the doors. Just before I got to the elevators, I could see Envy through a glass window as she sat in a very small room answering telephones. When she saw me, she smiled from ear to ear. I quickly went to the side door, and after she let me in, she told me to go sit in a chair behind a wall that separated her office from the hidden area where we would be fucking. It seemed to me that she must have done this many times before.

Envy had on a white blouse with a long green skirt that would provide easy access. She went as far as she could in the corner of the hidden spot in the small office. Without saying a word, I pulled my hard penis out of my pants and put it straight in her mouth. She sucked it slowly as my dick began to occupy her entire mouth. Envy said she loved a big penis, and I surely had a big one for her. I must have fucked her mouth for twenty strong minutes before I was ready to guide the motherfucker in her pussy. Once I rolled on a latex condom, I stuck that dick straight in her wet pussy. All you could hear was her releasing a loud grunt.

"Damn, that's a big dick, Dontaye. Fuck this pussy, baby. Fuck this pussy," Envy said as I hit it from the back.

Reaching my hand around her to the front, I started rubbing her clitoris while continuing to bang the dick in and out of her constantly. With no hands, my dick went from her pussy and jumped straight into her asshole. After fucking her for a good forty-five minutes, I released a large load of cum into her rectum, and I was done. I removed the rubber, flipped my soft dick back in my pants, gave her a kiss, and headed for the door.

"I'll call you later, boo," Envy yelled as I slid out the door.

I could tell Envy was a cold freak, and it's possible that she was the hospital hoe, but I loved every bit of it.

Chapter 8
THE CONTROL FACTOR

One thing my mother believed in was control. She always felt she must be the ruler in any situation. Either you're the player or the one being played. There are many ways to control a person. For example, you can control someone by their ego. People do not know that the ego is something you can always play on in more ways than one. If I told a person that someone said they were a snitch, and then that person killed the person who I said told me that, was it him that killed the person or was it his ego? Makes sense, doesn't it?

Well, I got a call from my mother one night, and she started telling me about the money my father was bringing in. She had also added three more male transsexual prostitutes to her stable of whores. She told me the names of her new male whores were Pearl, Terri, and Jackie. As I sat and listened to Rabbit, I could clearly understand that life is about survival, and running game is the way to make shit happen.

"Son, one thing I believe in is making these bitches get my money. I don't care if they got to take a dick as big as the Washington Monument. They better sit on the motherfucker and get that money. I don't play about my money," Rabbit said as I heard the sound of liquid being poured into a glass in the background.

I know my mother, and if that wasn't Remy Martin she was pouring, I'd be a monkey's uncle.

"What's that you drinking on, Mom? Remy Martin?"

"Dontaye, don't play with me, son. You know what the hell I'm drinking. It's not a game. You know them hoes better get me some Remy Martin," Rabbit screamed out.

She went on to tell me that her new transsexual hoes were bringing in good money and that she had been planning a big heist that would be the ultimate payday. One thing I can say about her is she's a true mastermind.

"Dontaye, always remember that you got to have guts. NO GUTS, NO GLORY! Always be willing to try something new. That's the only way you'll see what your hand calls for. People can't hold a person back. It's a person's thinking that holds them back. If you're dealing with a woman and you can't see no growth, or it's always an argument or problem, or she's always making statements like whatever you do is never enough or you're never right in her eyes, you got to let that bitch go. She has no loyalty to you, and she's trying to make you weak by creating a weakness in your manhood. Never go for shit like that, son," Rabbit said, then paused to take a sip of Remy Martin from her glass.

"So how are things going over there at the massage parlor?" she asked.

"It's going well. I need to get out and promote it more, but for the most part, it's doing well."

"Are you keepin' them bitches in line?"

"Yeah, Momma, I got everything in check."

I didn't want to mention anything about Sugar Momma because Rabbit always said never let people get too close or in your business. So, I kept the conversation basic and straight to the point. I'll never keep a secret from Rabbit, but I just wasn't ready to hear and feel the wrath from her about my being in that situation that went down with Sugar Momma and Solo.

Rabbit told me that she saw Johnny Black and Sonny Redz, and they had asked about me. In fact, they wanted to meet up with me because they had been hearing good things about me. That was a good thing to hear, especially from the elder pimps in the game. Most pimps in this business don't stay friends too long because rules are meant to be broken, and respect can quickly be lost. A pimp will knock your bitch as soon as she's willing to choose another pimp. It's no different than a wife or girlfriend cheating with another man or woman. She simply chose someone else. To be honest, it was good to know that the elder pimps wanted to meet up with me, but I knew it was hard to keep up in this game. The difference between them and me is I'm a businessman and they are street pimps. It's all business, but it's not always what you do, it's how you do it.

I was sure it would be a real pleasure to see Sonny Redz and Johnny Black. It would be official pimp business when we met, and as an upcoming businessman, I couldn't wait to get some of that good ole knowledge they have to pass down to a young brother like me. In life, we all will hear a lot, but what means the most is when you listen to someone who can make you dollars at the end of the day. You got to choose wisely who you listen to or believe in, because as always, you survive off of how good your game is in this business.

A couple weeks later, I met up with Sonny Redz and Johnny Black, and as always, they both were sharply dressed from head to toe.

"Hey pimpin'!" I yelled, while crossing busy 14th Street in northwest Washington D.C.

Sonny Redz and Johnny Black stood in front of a busy coffee shop near the middle of the block. As I walked up to the legendary pimps, they welcomed me with open arms.

"I've been hearing some good things about you, Dontaye, and it's a pimp's destiny to rise to the next level in which he came to rise. Continue to rise, young man. Continue to rise," Sonny Redz said as he hugged me with excitement.

"Yeah, Dontaye. It's good to hear that you stepped your game up and took pimpin' to another level. Not one...I mean, none of us players ever thought the change in the game was coming. No one has ever done it the way you're doing it, pimp. You might earn the Pimp of the Year for this game here, playa," Johnny Black said as he held out his hand for me to shake.

"So tell me, Dontaye. How's your business doing in this new area of pimpin'?" Sonny Redz asked with a slight cunning look on his face.

It seemed like I saw some slight hating in the both of them. I gave them the benefit of the doubt because looks can be deceiving, but I knew those looks anywhere. Too many people in the United States wear those same looks on their faces—the hater look. If you're from the United States of America, then you know what I'm talking about. No sense in faking it. Call a hater a hater. One thing about them foreigners, they stick together, but over here in the USA, we're the only race that does harm to each other. I often wonder when we're going to wake up.

Anyway, I replied with a great ball of energy, "The money is flowing in good, and the girls are on the grind. As long as it's all done with respect, I can't complain."

Although I had to be brief and to the point with them, I still kept it respectful because they were elder pimps. However, I didn't know what their motives were for wanting to meet up or inquiring about how good my business was doing. Some shit people don't ask about unless they got a plan. In this game, the players don't always play by the rules. If you got to watch your so-called friends and partners in the drug game, then what you think I got to do on this side of the fence. I'm making a lot of money, and I got the women who fuck other women to make sure they give them the nut they've been waiting so long to get. Pimps are going to hate on me all over the damn world. And you know what? Fuck 'em!

Chapter 9
THE BATTLE OF THE BELTWAY

The dancers of Secret Admire Entertainment were having a dance-off competition against a group of doms and fems from Richmond, Virginia, called Blazing Hot Entertainment at the Aqua Club on New York Ave NE. MC Dom Diva hosted the event, while DJ Betty B did her thing on the 1's and 2's. The lights were dimmed, and the colorful blue, red, green, and yellow lights shined on the glossy waxed stage floor.

"First coming to the stage is DC's own Swagga. Get your dollar bills ready for this hot, muscle-bound bodybuilder. I bet Swagga can fuck one of you fine-ass ladies good tonight. Go get 'em, Swagga," MC Dom Diva said on the microphone that echoed her words as she spoke.

As "One In a Million" by Aaliyah started to play, Swagga danced her way out of the dressing room donned in a black leather cowboy hat, a black leather tank top, and some black leather cowboy pants that had black leather tassels going down the sides of them. Once she hit the stage, Swagga pulled a fine, brown-skinned young woman out to the center of the floor by her hand and gently laid her down on her back. As the music continued to play, Swagga pulled up the woman's rainbow-colored mini skirt and put her entire head underneath it. Quickly, "What's Your Fantasy" by Ludacris was blended in, and all you could hear was the crowd singing, "I wanna lick, lick, lick, lick you from your head to your toes, and I wanna move from the bed down to the…down to the floor."

The crowd continued to sing as Swagga humped the woman and then flipped her over on to her stomach. As the woman laid there with her skirt up and her blue thongs showing, Swagga pulled a leather whip from the waist of her pants and began whipping the woman's buttocks. Several women from the audience walked up to them and started dropping one dollar bills on Swagga. One woman in particular walked up and dropped at least two hundred one dollar bills on them. In the clubs where the girls dance for girls, I must say that women tip better than men on any day of the week.

Before you knew it, the song was over and MC Dom Diva

was counting down. "10, 9, 8, 7, 6, 5, 4, 3, 2, and 1. I want to thank Swagga for coming out here all oiled up for the ladies. Show them stomach abs off with your strong self. You need to help me get in shape. Did you ladies know that Swagga is a personal trainer?" MC Dom Diva said as the next dancer prepared to hit the stage.

"We got a lovely young fem coming to the stage by the name of Dynomite from Blazin' Hot Entertainment. Everybody show her some love. Everybody get your dollar bills ready for this sexy little thang here. Damn, she got a nice ass on her. Look how that ass is shaking as she walks to the stage, y'all. Damn, I want some of that, boo. Can I have some of that, boo?" MC Dom Diva asked as she walked over to Dynomite.

Dynomite was about 4'9" and weighed about 130 pounds. She had a light brown complexion with shoulder-length black hair. The one thing I loved about Dynomite was those pretty blue eyes.

As Dynomite got on stage, "Crazy in Love" by Beyoncé featuring Jay-Z came on. Dynomite ran across the stage and flipped with no hands, then dropped to a wide split. As she rolled over on both hands and knees, she crawled over to a female that looked to be Spanish and pulled her out onto the floor. The young woman seemed to enjoy being the center of attention. As everyone watched, several females walked over to

Dynomite and dropped many dollar bills on both Dynomite and the Spanish woman as they humped, rubbed, and squeezed each other's sexy, soft bodies. Dynomite danced for about four minutes before MC Dom Diva started the countdown from the number ten down to number one, meaning that the dancer's time had expired on the stage.

During the countdown, Dynomite flipped the Spanish woman on her back and then over on to her stomach. The woman's dress flew up as she got on her hands and knees. She had the prettiest ass cheeks a young woman could ever have. Actually, I saw angel wings tattooed on her ass, one on each cheek. As Dynomite left the stage, the Spanish woman quickly pulled her dress down and vanished into the crowd of women.

Several dancers from Blazin' Hot Entertainment and Secret Admire Entertainment hit the stage, and as the competition came to an end, the judges started to compare their votes while some of the spectators got drinks from the bar and waited to hear the announcement of the winner. Others continued to party.

A few seconds before MC Dom Diva announced the winner, a small white woman walked up to her and asked if she could make a quick announcement. When MC Dom Diva handed her the microphone, the woman asked her lover to marry her. The woman's lover came over to her, and they kissed for about five long minutes before the lover finally said, "Yes, baby, I love you so much. I will marry you right now if you want me to."

"Wow! Did y'all see that?" MC Dom Diva said. "They're in love. That is so cute. I'ma ask my baby momma to marry me when I get home tonight. But, right now, I'm going to announce the winner of this competition." MC Dom Diva walked over to the judges' table. "And the winner is...Secret Admire Entertainment!" MC Dom Diva announced as she read from the judges' voting sheet. "Congrats to Secret Admire Entertainment. As always, it's been a really great show tonight, and y'all can come to the after-party. It's a closed door affair, where every woman in this motherfucker can get their titties sucked and their pussies eaten, and even eat some pussy if that's what you want to do. Whatever makes your boat float. Anything goes.

"Hey Dontaye! Dontaye! Is that Dontaye? Come over here, please. Hey, y'all, Dontaye got the bitches at his massage parlor. Get his card and go over to the massage parlor. It's a place you'll never forget, believe me," MC Dom Diva said on the microphone as I walked over to her.

"Hey, babes, what's up?" I said to MC Dom Diva, who had a fine-ass woman hugged up on her.

"Hey, Dontaye, I just wanted to let you know where the swingers' party is so you can be there. There are gonna be some fine women there for your stable. You might meet some that want to be clients or make that money for you. I just wanted to pull you up on that."

"I'ma be there. That's all I needed to know. Good looking out on that."

After hugging MC Dom Diva, I started walking towards the exit. On my way, I saw a lot of doms and fems hugged up. Some were in dark corners of the club kissing, while others were sitting on someone's lap. One thing I can say is everybody seemed to be having a nice time, and that's what meant the most.

As I got into my Mercedes Benz, two females ran up on me and asked did I have a number that they could reach me at. I handed them a business card and explained that in my line of business you must have a lot of hustle in you. Money is made and paid be the second, minute, and hour. I also explained that if they wanted the finer things in life, they had to be connected with the right people that could make great things happen.

Both women told me that they had heard about me and that one of their biggest dreams was to work for me. I was amazed that my name had started ringing, and it felt good inside to know that my hard work was paying off. Like the old saying goes, *What you put into something is what you're gonna get out of it.*

Chapter 10
GETTING IT IN

I decided to go to the after-party that MC Dom Diva told me about. When I hit the block, instantly I found the address. It was so many damn cars on the street that there wasn't a parking space to park.

"Shit, with all these damn cars, they must be having a good pussy fucking and sucking time in that motherfucker," I said, finally spotting a place to park on the partly lit street.

As I walked to the front door of the address that MC Dom Diva had given me, I noticed I could hear oooh's and ahhh's from what looked to be a bedroom window. I stood there for about ten minutes, and then I heard the loudest scream in ecstasy. Louder than some of what I've heard in the massage parlor. When I realized it seemed to be some major female fucking going on in that joint, I immediately knocked on the door, and I mean, I knocked hard as a motherfucker. See, they may have been just having a party, but this was the shit my business was made of. I mean, I count major paper off the shit they were doing for fun. So, I needed to get in there and recruit some workers AND some clients. You feel me? You must take control of or figure out how to capitalize on some things that fit into your line of expertise as fast as you can.

When I knocked on the door for the second time, a female slowly opened the door. I couldn't help but to notice that it was Big Mya, one of the female bodyguards who worked security for MC Dom Diva and the entire Secret Admire Entertainment. Big Mya didn't take no shit. Standing about six-feet, nine-inches and weighing about 300 pounds, she was very dark skinned and always wore black leather gloves that she would use to knock a bitch straight out, if necessary. Anyone who frequents the Delta will tell you that she doesn't play.

As I walked in the house, I gave Big Mya dap fist to fist. "What's up, Big Mya?" I asked.

"Nothing much. Just making sure everybody has fun and no problems start, and if so, I'll end it real quick," Big Mya replied, while cracking her knuckles on both hands.

I walked through the dining room to the living room and saw two air mattresses on the floor. There were three women to a mattress, butt-ass naked and sucking on each others' pussies like a female lion licking her newborn cub clean after birth. After walking through the whole downstairs, I started up the steps only to find more female fucking on the next level. I mean, they were taking sex to another level up there. Wow!

As I continued walking, I noticed just how heated the moment had become to them by the women's clothes that were scattered everywhere. There were underwear, bras, skirts, dresses, blouses, and I even saw panty liners. Everything a woman used I saw as I reached the narrow hallway.

There was a lot of bed squeaking and moaning coming from the four bedrooms. I even heard the sound of skin popping, like someone was getting fucked hard from the back. My attention shifted to the room at the end of the narrow hallway, where a lot of laughter and some giggling were coming from. If I had to guess what was actually taking place in that backroom, I wouldn't have thought it would be sex.

As I walked closer to the room, it seemed as if my steps started to get slower, like something was holding me back, but the noise from the room got louder. When I finally got to the room, I could see a light because the door was slightly cracked open. Taking a peek through the tiny crack of the door, I saw three young black women inside the room. One woman was tied up with a rope made from a clothesline and lying on her back with both legs spread wide open, while a second woman was choking her around the neck. The other woman was constantly sucking her pussy to a no count. I mean, this woman was giving that woman some mean-ass head. The noise I took to be laughter was actually the sounds of the woman gasping for air from being choked so damn hard.

I didn't move a bit, because I had never seen anyone choke a sex partner until they passed out like this woman had just done. I mean, this bitch was out cold, but the young woman continued eating the woman's pussy as if she was lying there conscious and watching her. The woman stopped choking her and started watching the woman as she licked and sucked away on the unconscious woman.

Suddenly, I heard the unconscious woman moan, and then I could see her head turn from side to side. Slowly, I could see her moving her hips in a circular motion like she was fucking. For another ten minutes or so, I watched the woman suck that pussy until the other woman, who had been the chocker, strapped on a thick, long dildo and began to penetrate the barely unconscious woman's vaginal entrance.

For another fifteen minutes, the woman fucked her pussy until I saw beads of sweat on both women's foreheads. Unexpectedly, the woman began to release her sweet juices by the squirt full, like she was pissing urine. When the unconscious woman started to wake up, the other woman jumped up and sat her clean-shaven pussy straight in her face and right on her mouth. Without hesitating, the young woman began licking the long clitoris and then graduated to thrusting her tongue in and out of the tight pussy hole of the horny, young woman.

I couldn't help but notice that the three women were taking sex to a higher level. I mean, it's like they actually got high off the sex they were having. I was so amazed by the sexual experience they possessed that I had to see what was going to happen next.

Don't get me wrong. I witnessed women having sex all the time at the massage parlor, but I knew I needed to have these ladies on standby in case any of my girls started to change up on me. I really didn't know what end of my plan they would fall in, but I did know I had room for them on either side of the plan.

I walked to another door that was to the left of the room I was just standing at, turned the doorknob, and walked in. There were four white women in that room. Two of them were on their hands and knees on a couch. The other two had on strap-on dildos and were fucking them from behind. That was the loud noise of skin popping that I'd had heard earlier as I walked past the room.

Taking a seat on another couch that was inside the room, I watched as they fucked their little hearts out. Twenty minutes later, the show came to an end. I gave the four women my cards and told them if they'd like to make a lot of money, then they needed to give me a call.

I didn't stay at the party long. In fact, after giving out my cards to some of the ladies as they began coming out of the many rooms that were occupied, I returned to my business.

Chapter 11
SUCCESS HAS ENEMIES

I went back to the massage parlor to see how things had been since I was gone. The girls were doing what they do best—on dates and getting that money. I sat down at my desk, looked at the monitors, and saw that three of my doms—Fantasy, Fame, and Rainbow—had a client that they were all running a train on. The client was a white woman who stood about 5'5" and had a nice phat ass on her. She looked to be about twenty-three years old, and she was one gorgeous woman.

The doms had her ass in many different positions. Fantasy and Fame both fucked her with big black dildos, taking turns as the young woman screamed out in pleasure. Rainbow decided to just let the woman eat her pussy until she came a few times. From what I saw, the bitch wanted sex, and my girls just burned her pussy up and broke her ass down.

Anyway, I turned the monitor off and decided to talk to the fems about some important things that needed to be dealt with. As I gathered them together, my cell phone rang. It was an old friend of mine from back in junior high school named Boga Miller. He was a good dude when we were in school. As a matter of fact, he was my best friend back in those days.

"Hello," I answered.

"Hey, Dontaye. This is Boga Miller, man. What's up partner?" Boga Miller said loudly into the telephone.

"Hey, Boga. What's happening, slim? What you been up to?" I asked, glad to hear from him.

"Man, I just thought I'd give you a call since we exchanged numbers the other day. I'm trying to catch up with you soon. What's a good day or time?"

"We can catch up today, if you want. Meet me at the Penthouse Strip Club at six o'clock," I told him.

"It's about three o'clock now, so that's a good time. I'll see you there at six, Dontaye."

"Okay, Boga, I'll see you then," I told him, then pressed the button to end the call. "Okay, girls, it's time to have a meeting. I just need to say that y'all have been doing great on making that money. Things are looking so good that I'm going to take everyone on a shopping spree. I'm gonna spend one thousand dollars on each one of y'all tomorrow."

Excited, the girls hugged and kissed my handsome face.

"Is there anything we need to talk about before I leave?" I asked them.

Wet Wet raised her hand and started to speak. "Sugar Momma called and told me that she wanted to take me out to dinner. I told her that I didn't think you'd like that, but she went on to say for me not to worry about what you might or might not like because it's about her and what she likes. I didn't say anything. I just said okay and let it go," Wet Wet informed me.

"Oh yeah? She went like that? We'll see about that," I said, while dialing Sugar Momma's number.

As I put my cell phone up to my ear, I could hear Sugar Momma's phone ring several times. To be honest, my heart started to beat faster with each ring, because I knew, without a doubt, that Sugar Momma would kill me or have someone else to kill me if I got on her bad side. So, I had to be very careful on how I dealt with her about the situation.

Don't get it twisted. I'm no punk, and I'm not scared of her. It's just that I felt I needed to be smarter than her about the situation, though. From what I'd heard in the streets, many people had lost their lives to this woman by not thinking first before reacting.

"Hello, who the fuck is this? A bitch is tryin' to sleep right now," she answered.

"Hey, Sugar Momma, it's Dontaye. Can we talk for a moment?"

"Sure. What's on your mind, partner?" she replied.

Instantly, I felt confused. I didn't know what else to say or do because her response didn't sound negative. It seemed as if my mind was playing tricks on me. Now, I knew Wet Wet wouldn't lie to me, but it didn't seem like Sugar Momma was trying to knock me for one of my girls. Instead of saying something about what I was told, I decided to just act as if I was checking up on her.

"Hey, babes, I was thinking about you because I haven't heard from you. What you been up to?" I asked.

"I've been trying to get at that bitch, man. Ever since she shot my muthafuckin' windows out, I been tryin' to see that stink cock bitch!" Sugar Momma screamed. "The bitch be wearing all types of disguises, from wigs and sunglasses to fake body hair like a moustache and beard. She's a sneaky bitch that can't be slept on. I got to lay her ass down," Sugar Momma explained calmly.

"I'm with you, babes. Look, if you need me to roll with you, I'm down," I said, even though I wanted no part of the beef between her and Solo.

The only reason I even said it was to make her think I was

on her team. That way, I would look good in her eyes and just maybe she wouldn't try to knock me for Wet Wet or any of my other girls.

"Thanks, Dontaye, but this is personal. I'ma take this bitch out myself. I got some high-powered artillery," she said.

I was so glad to hear that she was going to kill Solo herself, because I had money to make and didn't have no time for trouble.

That was some deep shit between them. It was strange to see two women go that damn hard at each other. Although Solo's mother was killed and Sugar Momma's drugs were stolen, there had to be more to the story. Personally, I think those bitches were fucking each other, as well.

While talking to Sugar Momma for another hour and a half, she started telling me about her going to the Crossroads Night Club the other night. She said there was a nice crowd and the ladies were looking real good. She even told me that she met a pretty-ass woman in there who let her fingerfuck her in a dark corner of the club.

After Sugar Momma and I finished talking, I went uptown to the Penthouse Strip Club to meet up with Boga Miller.

Chapter 12

THE SIMPLEST THINGS

As we may know, the simplest things in a relationship can mean so much to someone. When I met Envy for the first time, I had a feeling come over me that I never knew. Have you ever seen someone that you were attracted to as soon as you looked at them? Not to mention, if you started a conversation with them and they acted just as interested in you as you are in them. That's a good feeling, and we will do almost anything to keep those feelings.

Well, my reason for saying this is because I was never the type of guy that would go out of my way to express my inner feelings to a woman, even in my teenage years. Yet, I knew with Envy it would have to be different. Whenever I was in her presence, it seemed that my soul was melting like butter, and I knew I would do whatever was necessary to keep this woman close.

Since Envy and I met, we've talked on the telephone many nights for several weeks, and each night we talked, we would bond even tighter than we were the night before.

Anyway, I received a call from Envy on a Saturday morning, and the sound of her voice reminded me of the sweet sound of melodies. She was music to my ears.

"Good morning, sweetie. I hope you had the thought of me held close to your heart as you slept last night," Envy said.

"Hey, sweetheart, you know I did, babes. How are you feeling this morning?" I asked, while thinking of the many ways I could show this woman nothing but my true love.

"I'm feeling like being with you today. That's how I'm feeling. What about you, Dontaye?"

"Baby, I'm feeling the same way. I'm feeling like being with you. Not just today, but forever."

"Awww, Dontaye, that was so sweet of you to say. I want to be with you forever, too, honey," Envy said.

The closer Envy and I became the more I realized she would eventually want to know what type of work I did for a living, but I knew that probably should never happen.

Later that evening, slightly before sundown, Envy and I went out to have dinner at Tony and Joe's Seafood Restaurant in Georgetown. Three boats and a yacht docked about fifteen feet away from the table where we sat outside. About five minutes had passed before an attractive white waitress with blonde hair came over to take our orders. I ordered the seafood platter, and she ordered soft-shell crabs.

As we sat at the table, I got up close on Envy and gave her a long, sweet kiss while gazing straight into her sexy eyes. We enjoyed every second of every moment together, and there was not a tenth of a second wasted.

After eating, we decided to take a walk through the park. She felt soft to me as I touched her body from head to toe. With my tongue as far back in her throat as I could get it, I'm quite sure she could feel the thickness of my growing hard dick up against the middle of her stomach. At that point, we decided to leave the park and go get into some hardcore lovemaking.

As soon as we got into my car, Envy leaned over, pulled my thick, long, crooked dick out my pants, and started sucking it like porn star Pinky does in her many porn flicks. The way Envy sucked a dick, I was sure she was going be in my life for many years to cum.

Chapter 13
ALWAYS BE ACCOUNTABLE
FOR YOUR TIME

I had to keep in mind that I was now making money like a motherfucker. This new era of prostitution that's called escorting erases the old images of a black man beating up on a woman for not giving him all her money or giving money to him period, especially after she just sucked a dick or fucked a man in an alley somewhere.

Anyway, I decided to go on the track where Momma pimps her male prostitutes. As I drove onto the block, I saw a marked police car. I couldn't see who it was until I got a little closer. It was Officers Burrell and Smith. As I rode past them, I met eyes with Officer Smith aka Red Devil.

"Hey, boy, pull that damn car over. We've been looking for you," Red Devil said.

I didn't know if I should stop the car or keep it moving. Soon, I noticed their flashing red and blue lights along with the loud siren as the car turned around to follow me. Once I pulled over to the curb near 12th and N Streets in northwest D.C., Officers Smith and Burrell jumped out the police car with their guns drawn, ordering me out of my Mercedes Benz. As I got out, I put my hands up in the air and asked what the problem was.

"Dontaye, get your ass on the ground!" Red Devil yelled.

I dropped to the ground so that whatever the problem was it wouldn't get any worse. As I lay on my stomach, Officer Burrell walked up and put his knee in my back while placing the handcuffs on me. I didn't have the slightest idea what I was being arrested for, but there was nothing I could do.

They put me in the marked police car and took me down to police headquarters. When I got there, I was turned over to these two detectives. They told me their names, but I was so confused about my situation that I didn't hear them. I was trying to figure out what was going on.

After I sat in a small room for about an hour, the same two detectives walked in and started questioning me about a murder that happened three months ago. They said some informants told them that Rabbit and I were seen during the time a murder took place in a nearby alleyway at 13th and L Streets. They also said the deceased man was a transgender male who happened to be a prostitute. They showed me pictures of the man, whose throat was cut from ear to ear. I told the detectives that I had not been around that area for a very long time and that I had never seen that man a day in my life.

When asked if I knew where they could find Rabbit, I told the short, black, chubby detective, "I haven't seen my mother in about a month or so."

The other detective was a tall white man who seemed like he didn't believe anything I said. He asked me for Rabbit's telephone number and address, and I told him that I didn't have either.

"Now I'm supposed to believe that you don't know your own mother's address or telephone number? You must think we're fools!" the white detective screamed.

They told me that they knew my mother pimped male prostitutes and that she was a violent woman who didn't take any shit. They also told me that they had been hearing things about me, as well, but they never said what they had heard. I really didn't trip off of what they were saying, though. However, I did take in everything so I could better cover my tracks from here on out.

They interviewed me for several more hours, and at about three o'clock in the morning, they finally decided they didn't have enough to charge me for murder at the time. As I walked out the door and down a very long hallway with the short, chubby detective, he explained to me that this was an investigation. Therefore, if they found probable cause, they would charge me and my mother with murder, and a search warrant would be issued for the both of us.

"Just because we're letting you walk out of here this time doesn't mean it's over. I want you to remember that. If you want to talk, here's my card. I can help you if you want to tell me something," he said as I walked out the police headquarters without saying a word.

Chapter 14

ADMITTING YOU'RE WRONG DOESN'T MEAN YOU'RE ADMITTING TO YOUR STUPIDITY

S ome people will never admit they are wrong. Some people believe admitting they're wrong is admitting that they are stupid. Sometimes, getting someone to admit they're wrong is like pulling teeth out a motherfucker's mouth. I can't do anything but laugh at those types of people, because they are the sneaky, mentally ill ones.

One day, I ran into a friend of mine named Jimmy Tank in front of Howard University Hospital. We were both glad to see each other because it had been a minute since we had talked. We shook hands as we greeted each other, and it was a real pleasure to see him. Jimmy Tank is the type of person who always had something to say that you could learn from. This day, he started telling me some shit about his baby's mother.

"Dontaye, my baby's mother is one lying-ass bitch. She's the type of female that brings nothing but confusion and lies to a relationship," he told me.

"Why do you say that? She seems to be cool from the few times I've seen her. As a matter of fact, I saw her out here a couple days ago talking to some dude out here," I said, thinking back to the last time I saw her.

"That's the shit I'm talking about. I've heard that she's been creeping around the hospital with a married guy that be fucking her in back rooms and shit. And the trip part about it is the nigga don't give her nothing but a dick and a dream," Jimmy Tank said, as we both laughed at the hoe.

"So how did you meet her?" I asked.

"I met the lying bitch at her people's house about eight years ago. She was cheating with me on her last baby's father. She just wanted to fuck me, so I put the dick in her. She ain't want shit then. She seemed cool in the beginning, but as I got to know her, I realized she was just another lying-ass hoodrat," Jimmy Tank said, looking heartbroken.

"When you deal with a female that will never admit she's wrong, you must remember that she will stick with a lie just as strong. I'm going to tell you something else about her. She's the type that's so miserable that she wants me and everyone else to be miserable, too. Have you ever dealt with a female that you were glad to be with when y'all got together, but then she had to say something fucked up to make you mad while you with her? She's that type of broad. She's a smart-mouth, miserable-ass, scorned bitch. Her mother is the same way, and she raised her to be that way. I learned my lesson from her ass. If I ever meet another woman like her, I'm going to run like hell," he told me. "Every slick-ass broad like them gets nothing but a drink, a dick, and a dream for thinking they are so damn slick," he added.

When Jimmy Tank told me about his baby's mother and the shit she did to keep drama started, I immediately thought about what Pimpin' Ken said about a burned-out hoe. *She's miserable and wants everyone around her to be miserable.* The reason these women are like that is because they're fucked up mentally. They were raised fucked up and were taught nothing but fucked-up things. On top of it all, their time has expired and they know it. They know a man isn't going to take them seriously. You can't reverse the bad habits and immoral principles they were taught. They're fucked up, and they know it. They'll try to make it look like it's you with the problem to keep the focus off of them.

If you ever come across a female like Jimmy Tank's baby's mother, make sure you leave the bitch as soon as you notice her fucked-up behavior. Make sure you're able to recognize that type when you see her, because it will save you from having to deal with a bunch of headaches and stressful, stupid shit. I forgot the name of the phobia they suffer from, but those bitches are weird! Real talk!

Chapter 15

1-900-GET YOUR PUSSY SUCKED

I decided to step my game up because the game is always a hustle, no matter what your drop is. I still had my escort service, but investing in a sex chat line for lesbians was my new drop. Life means surviving, and surviving means to work your game. The world we live in is a big ole game we're playing. Either you're playing a motherfucker or you're getting played, plain and simple. That's why you got to have a NO EXCUSES NECESSARY lane. That means you must have an area in your business that's off limits to everyone, even close friends and family. Keep your cards as close to your chest as possible, if you know what I mean.

Anyway, I set up an account with the telephone company to start my own lesbian chat line for doms or fems, whatever you like. Since MC Dom Diva was well-known in the lesbian/gay community, I hired her to be the voice of the doms. I started searching around for my first fem voice, but that didn't happen until I went to see Lil' Porsche perform at Club Ibiza one night.

When I walked in the door, the dance floor was crowded, just as any club owner would want it to be. I mean, there were sexy women everywhere. All I saw was short skirts with sexy asses. I was on the hunt for the right woman that could model for my ad and be the spokeswoman for my chat line. So, I walked through the club scouting for that special woman. After being in the club for about an hour and a half, I finally saw who I was looking for—a beautiful woman standing with two other fine-ass women. She couldn't have been more than twenty-four years old. The woman was brown skinned, had long black hair, stood about five-feet, six-inches tall, and weighed about 135 pounds. She had the fattest ass a person would want to see. Believe me!

"Hello, Miss Lady, I couldn't help but notice that you're the most beautiful woman in this club."

"Thank you," she replied.

"My name is Dontaye, and I'd like to know if you would be interested in modeling for my company?" I asked her.

"I'm Kitten. What kind of company do you have?"

"I have an entertainment company that makes a lot of money. I would really like you to work for my company. You have the look that I've been searching for, and I can pay you a lot of money for that look," I told the seductive-looking woman.

While handing her one of my business cards, I told her to give me a call when she left the club or the next day whenever she was free. She looked at me as if I was the man she had been looking for all her damn life. The word MONEY is a bad motherfucker! I decided I would have a little fun while I was there and meet as many females as I could, because if there's one thing I knew, it was that females make you money. To my knowledge, having females on your team is always a plus if you know what you're doing.

I danced a little bit, had a drink of Sprite, watched a few females, and got my freak on. When I received a call from the massage parlor, it was time to go.

"Hello. What's up?" I asked.

"Dontaye, Nikita Sunshine and Rainbow are fighting. You need to get here as soon as possible," Princess said loudly into the telephone.

"What's the problem? Why are they fighting?"

"I don't know, but I think they've been fucking with each other."

Now, I really didn't want the girls to have any relationships between each other, but there was nothing I could really do about it if they did. However, I knew being sexually involved with someone that you worked with would only cause problems, and I didn't need anyone's problems bringing attention to my new hustle.

After telling Princess to calm things down until I got there, I drove as fast as I could, and about twenty minutes later, I was walking up the steps and into the massage parlor. Rainbow and Nikita Sunshine were sitting on a couch in the waiting area as I walked through the door.

"Hey, what's going on between y'all? We don't need any problems or attention from the police," I stated.

Rainbow spoke up first. "I just had a fucked-up day and couldn't control my emotions, that's all. I'm alright now."

While looking her straight in the eye, I said, "Now, I really don't want y'all to have any relationships between each other, but if you can keep your personal beefs between the two of you, then I don't have a problem with it."

They reassured me the problem was over and that it wouldn't happen again. Still, just to be sure everything was settled, I decided to stick around at the massage parlor and wait to see if I would hear from Kitten.

Calls started coming in and business picked up from about 12:45 a.m. until 7:00 a.m. I must have made about eight thousand dollars in that time period. So, I took everyone to breakfast to reward them for their hard work. While eating, we talked about the new drop in my hustle, the sex chat line.

I told the girls that I hired MC Don Diva to be the voice for the dom and was waiting on Kitten to give me a call for the voice of the fem. They thought it was a good idea, and they expressed an interest in being the voice from time to time, as well. I really didn't see anything wrong with their suggestion, but I wanted to get that side of my new hustle tight before doing any experimenting.

I already was making a very handsome amount of money daily from the escort business and paying each of my girls $3,000 a week, not to mention how much I would make with the chat line. I would be killing it in the game.

Finally, we finished eating and took a stroll through Georgetown. As we walked from store to store buying outfits and other things, my cell phone rang.

"Hello, may I speak with Dontaye."

"Who's this?" I asked.

"It's Kitten, the one you met at Ibiza last night."

"Oh, okay. What's up, babes? I want you to come to my office at about three o'clock, if you can make it," I told her.

"Okay, I can be there at that time."

"Great. I'll see you then." Before hanging up, I gave her the address to the massage parlor.

Later that afternoon, Kitten showed up about five minutes

early, which was a good look for beginners.

Knock! Knock! Knock! I walked swiftly to the front door and opened it to see the fine, sweet, young woman that I had met at Club Ibiza standing there.

"Kitten, I'm glad you made it. Come in so I can show you around and explain what we do here to service our community. You'll make a lot of money, and the job will be a piece of cake, believe me."

I walked Kitten through the entire massage parlor. She met each and every one of the girls, doms and fems. I explained everything to her and told her that she would be the voice of the fems for the chat line. She had no problem with her new job, and at that point, she wanted to know when she could start working.

"Okay, Kitten, I like that you're anxious to start working, but you got to remember that you're fulfilling the caller's fantasy. You have to make love to them over the telephone. You have to be whatever the caller wants you to be. Just remember that you're the feminine one on the line."

The chat lines were all hooked up, and we were ready to take our first caller at exactly 5:00 p.m. I had promoted my new chat line service in the city paper for three weeks prior to opening the lines. I posted the 1-900 numbers along with the date and time that everyone could start calling. It was good I met Kitten at the time I did because she could jump right in and use that sexy voice of hers to make the dollars roll in.

As Kitten sat at her desk with her headset on, it wasn't long before the calls started pouring in. About ten calls came in, but Kitten could only answer one of them at a time. The price of each call was $2.99 per minute, and the first caller talked for thirty minutes. This caused the other callers to either hung up or keep calling back over and over again.

"Hello, I'm your kitty cat. Kitten on the line. What's your name?"

"I'm Melissa. How are you?"

"The kitty cat is fine. I just need some loving. Can I ride that fat dick of yours, Melissa?" Kitten asked.

"Sure, baby, that's why I'm calling. First, I want to eat your pussy and lick your clit with my pointed tongue, then trace a figure-eight above your clitoral hood and loop around the base of your clit. Will that get your pussy warm and wet, honey?" Melissa asked.

"Yes, baby. Come and lick me with your best lick. I want you to reverse that figure-eight motion after you do it about ten more times, baby," Kitten said as she lifted up her skirt, put her right hand down in her underwear, and started rubbing her pussy.

Kitten asked me to cut the lights out so she could feel the

part and get into the role.

"Melissa, stick your middle finger up in my pussy and fingerfuck me while you lick my pussy in that circular motion. Try to hit my G-spot while you're fingerfucking me, baby. Fingerfuck me a little faster, baby, while you lick this pussy.

"Oh shit, baby. Oh shit. You feel my wetness? That's it. Can you taste it now? My juices are flowing out now, boo. I'm cumming! I'm cumming, baby! Now suck it all in your mouth, Melissa. Suck it up. Suck up all my cum because you're a nasty bitch!" Kitten said while fingering herself.

Melissa and Kitten had great phone sex as they went back and forth with having the hottest chat sex I've ever heard. The caller left the line after Kitten bust her nut, and then it was time for the next caller.

"Hey, this is Kitten on the line. What's your fantasy?"

"Hey, baby, I want to do some hardcore fucking and sucking tonight, but first, describe yourself to me," caller number two asked.

"Okay, well, I'm a sexy caramel complexion with long black hair down my back, and I have brown eyes. My ass is phat like the female rapper Trina. My pussy is tight and juicy with pink lips, and it's always ready to cum," Kitten said with a smile.

"Oh, that sounds good to me. What does your butthole look

like, boo. I want to fuck you in the ass. Can you take my nine-inch dick in your ass, Kitten?" the female caller uttered.

"I love dick in my ass, baby. I also like to have my asshole licked while I rub on my clit. That's the best feeling in the world. That makes me cum hard," Kitten said softly into the telephone.

"I'm stroking this big ole strap-on, honey. I got the Johnson's baby oil, and I'm beating this motherfucker like I'm doing hard time in a federal penitentiary, baby. I'm 'bout to cum in a minute. Put your finger in your butt, Kitten, and push it in and out until I cum. Shit! Shit! Shit! I'm cumming as I beat this motherfucker. I'ma cum on your butt, boo. Open your cheeks so I can cum inside that ass. Damn, Kitten, I came. I'm sweating like a motherfucker, too. I'm good now, boo. I'm going to take a shower, lay back, and go to sleep. I'll call you tomorrow. Thanks, baby," the female caller said before disconnecting the call.

Over a four-hour period, about six callers tied the lines up as Kitten mentally seduced each one into sexual bliss. MC Dom Diva came in ready to start work as the voice for the doms. The telephone rang, and it was time to start the show.

"Hello, this is the one and only MC Dom Diva. What's your fantasy tonight? If you want the dick, I'm ready to give it to you. Just open your mouth and let me slide it on in and down the back of your throat. I can make you fems out there feel real good tonight. How are you feeling, sweetheart?" MC Dom Diva asked.

"Hello, MC Dom Diva. I watched you dance at the DeLa Swan last night, and you're the bomb. I've seen you dance many times when you're not hosting the parties. I like how you had the strap-on dildo with the thick chain around your neck. That made me so hot that cum just started running out my pussy and into my underwear," the caller said.

"Oh yeah, I got that big ole dick in my hand now. You want to suck it for a little while, boo?"

"Yes, anything for you, MC Dom Diva. You can put your dick in my mouth, if you want. Just slide it up and down my clit for a while until my pussy gets soaking wet. This pussy is yours."

"You shouldn't have told me that, because I'm going to treat you with something real special tonight. I'm getting my mouth chilled with some ice. Open your legs, baby, and let me slide my chilled tongue along your clit. You feel it, boo? Ahh, I got a small piece of ice on my tongue. Now, I'ma gently press the ice against your labia and roll it around. If it feels good to you, rub your naked pussy with your hand. Rub your clit over and over again for me. Is it ready to cum or do you need my warm mouth on it because the ice is gone? Let me lick that pussy. Move your hand gotdamn it! I got a big dick, too, and I can fuck you all night long!" MC Dom Diva said loudly.

"I'm cumming, Dom Diva! My juices are squirting. I'm squirting out. I'm rubbing my clit fast with my left hand and fingerfucking my hole with my right. Damn, your dick is good. I came hard," the caller said, and then there was only silence after her orgasm.

I sat there with Kitten and MC Dom Diva until about one o'clock that afternoon. We were all tired, and it was time to sleep since we had been up all night. The girls and I usually slept at the massage parlor when we pulled many hours, so I didn't see anything wrong with Kitten and MC Dom Diva doing the same thing. I pulled out three air mattresses, set them up in a private room, and we fell asleep as if we had been working construction on a brand-new office building downtown or something. We were tired as shit.

I liked my new drop. I started out running a massage parlor, and one hustle turned into two. That's what it's all about— making moves. As one of my old partners Robert Mercer would say, IT'S NOT A GAME!

Chapter 16
LOVE IS THE GREATEST

About eight months had passed, and Envy and I were officially a couple. I loved her with all my heart. I never thought I could love a woman so damn hard.

"I'm so addicted to her that I can't even see straight," I said to myself, while walking from room to room in her large apartment.

Since having moved in with her, I felt my life had changed for the better, although I still ran my escort business. She didn't know how I made my money, and she never asked. Maybe she thought I was a drug dealer or just maybe she didn't give a fuck.

Envy was a very romantic woman, but I was just as romantic. On Sunday night, we laid in bed and read a book to each other. It was one of her favorite books—*Diary of a Thug.*

We read the entire book to each other, and that was romantic itself. A lot of men aren't romantic to their ladies, and that's mistake number one. If you don't take in consideration that a woman's heart and mind needs to be passionately shown affection, she'll eventually grow to hate you.

Since I knew that, I had to stay on top of my game. I would do things like write "I LOVE YOU, ENVY!" on each egg in the carton. So, when she opened the carton of eggs to cook them for breakfast, it would make her day to see that I took the time to make her day special from the very beginning. Being that she worked at Greater Southeast Hospital, I would send her fruit from the Edible Arrangements store on Allentown Rd. One night after we had some hardcore sex, I got up the next morning, went to a nearby store, purchased a case of matches, wrote the words "YOU LIGHT MY FIRE, BABY!" on the case, and mailed them to her address.

When I got home later that night, we had a candlelight dinner in the middle of the floor. Envy had on a crotchless black bodysuit so her fat, juicy pussy sat out for me to lick and suck until it got soaking wet. She had prepared stuffed lobster tails with crab meat and shrimp. It was a dish she had learned how to make from the world famous Mo's Seafood Restaurant in Baltimore.

As we ate, we played and told old jokes that we had heard

when we were kids. I felt so good inside that I fell in love with her much more. That night, I wanted to give Envy the best oral sex in town. I had learned so much from the girls at the massage parlor that I could be arrested and charged with assault on a female organ. My head is just that damn good.

"Envy, tonight, we're not using sex toys. My tongue will be your toy. You can use it anyway, anyhow, and anywhere you want."

"Okay, baby. That's why I love you so much. You know just what to say and do to turn me on," Envy replied.

I grabbed her into my arms and carried her to our bedroom. Once there, I laid back on the bed with my head back and stuck out my tongue. Envy grabbed the bedpost, squatted over top of my head, and put her shaved pussy up to my mouth. I gave her the steady tongue technique. I stuck my tongue out and let her have her way with it. For a few minutes, I did nothing but sit back and let her slip and slide all over my tongue. Then it was my turn to put things in motion. I let her guide my head and tell me how fast or how slow to go as I licked and sucked her pussy. Envy began to hold her head and play with her hair as I licked her pussy. As she neared an orgasm, she started screaming and moving real fast on my tongue.

"Oh yeah! Oh shit! Damn, that's it, Dontaye. Go in and out of my pussy with that tongue, baby. That's it, boo. Shit! Damn!

I got it. I'm cumming! I'm cumming! Awww!"

I guided Envy's head to my long, hard cock and slammed it straight down her throat. She sucked my horse-size cock like a professional porn star that had left the filming set to go home and make love to her man's throbbing cock. Envy was great at sucking dick, and to fuck her was out of this world. We made love all night, and it's always what we expect it to be—THE BOMB!

Love is the triumph of imagination over intelligence. It's funny to me how people think that being romantic somehow means something other than being yourself. What we all want is the spark, the magic, the thrill of love. The experience we all had at the beginning of our relationships. If feelings change, it can always be recreated through romance. With Envy in my life, I planned to keep our romantic flame burning forever.

A few days later, I sent Envy one rose to her job. I wrote a little note to her that said, "This bud's for you!" I always send surprise gifts to Envy at work, and most of the women either sit back admiring my game or hating on her. But, it doesn't matter, because as I see it, my game is on one hundred and their men need to catch up to me. If you want to keep your woman, keep her flattered, take care of her, and keep her happy. If you do these things, you can't lose.

Chapter 17
THE ROLES HAVE SWITCHED

Envy's friend Juicy owned a beauty salon in Laurel, Maryland, called Nikki's Place. Because Envy is a high-maintenance type of woman, she goes to the salon every week to keep her hair with that high-quality look.

One Saturday morning, Envy asked me to go with her to Nikki's Place to get her hair done. I had no problem with that, because I would do anything for this woman just to please her. If she asked me to walk through hell and back, I would do it. I loved myself some Envy, and I never saw this coming.

Even though I had several women working for me as escorts, I still learned a lot by holding a position such as mine. As a man, it's my job to understand a woman because it's how I make my money, and because I service the public in this way, I must know all the right things to say out of my mouth. The game has changed. Nowadays, women have reversed the game. Back in the day, most men had 3 or 4 women as girlfriends and side chicks to fuck. But now, the women have 3 or 4 men and boyfriends or females they fuck on the side. Yes, the game has been rewritten by the female.

We, as men, can't be mad, because at some point, the unconscious has to awaken to a conscious state. If you expose a woman to hurt and pain by the mistakes you make, at some point she can only learn from your mistakes. Then guess what? The rabbit has the gun, and the hunter has been captured by the game. A woman is an investment. If you catch her at the right time, she can be a great asset, but if she's filled with the wrong ingredients, it will be at a disadvantage for you to invest your time or money in her. It will only be an ugly disaster. That's why it is important for you as a man or woman, no matter what side of the game you're on, to KEEP YOUR GAME TIGHT!

If she likes to hear sweet things, tell her sweet things. If she likes flowers and love notes, give her that. If she likes her pussy ate out the frame and fucked with a big dildo, give it to her. And if she wants you to shower her with gifts and make her feel good even if she isn't, ALWAYS MAKE HER FEEL VERY SPECIAL!

Envy knew she was special to me. She understood that each second that went by in our life together was moving lightening fast, like a jet moving through the blue skies. We did everything together, and that's how it should be. She was the one that lit my path for me in my time of darkness.

Chapter 18
PROMOTIONS ARE EVERYTHING

It was time that I took the business to another level. I had to start promoting Big D Entertainment like I owned a Fortune 500 company. It was no joke. I called a buddy of mine named Bill who owned a photography studio over in Iverson Mall right off of Branch Avenue. I was told by some smart business owners that I could take Big D Entertainment to another level if I promoted it like an upcoming modeling agency as well as an entertainment company. So, I decided to have the girls do a photo shoot for posters and flyers that would be posted all around the D.C., Maryland, and Virginia area. I knew if I promoted the girls the right way, everything would fall right in place and money would be the least of my worries.

The photo shoot got underway about 5:45 p.m., and we started with the doms. Fantasy went first, wearing an all black

Versace suit, a white shirt, a black bowtie, black socks, and a pair of black and white hornback crocodile shoes. The first photo was a simple pose where she held the suit jacket over her shoulder with one finger. Then she had the entire suit on and stood as though she was handing a yellow daisy to the camera. Fantasy posed like she had been hired by the Versace clothing company herself.

Next, Nia Luv stepped into the spotlight and took over the photo shoot in her own little way. The thing about Nia Luv is she's the type that would stand out in any situation, especially in front of a camera. I knew with Nia Luv in front of the camera, it would be a piece of cake for her to give me the look I wanted. Nia Luv had on a blue jean jacket with nothing underneath and pants made by the Guess Jeans. Nia Luv sat at a large desk smoking a cigar, while Bill took about twenty-five pictures. She really gave us what we were looking for.

Ghetto Storm, the wild one in the bunch, wore tall green fishing boots up to her knees with a pair of green Hanes boxers. She had on a green sports bra with green boxer-like tape on each hand. Ghetto Storm stood in front of the camera as Bill took another twenty-five pictures. She threw punches like a true champion. You couldn't tell whether she was about to fight for the World Boxing Championship title or not.

Fame and Rainbow took their photo shoot together.

Rainbow stood in front of the camera with a short black bear fur jacket and nothing else on besides a strap-on dildo. Fame stood next to her dressed in a sheer, body-hugging cat suit and with a strap-on dildo hanging from her private area. Bill took about twenty-five pictures or more of them as they posed creatively, but freaky all around the studio.

Bill suggested all the doms pose together for the last picture. Fantasy, Ghetto Storm, Nia Luv, Fame, and Rainbow all stood together and gave us just what we needed—ONE HOT MOTHERFUCKIN' PICTURE!

Next up were my fems, and they were ready to go. Princess was the first to step in front of the camera. She had on a pink bra with matching pink underwear, and she was looking as fine as she could ever be. She took many pictures, as well.

Doneesha was after Princess, and once she stepped in front of the camera, the studio got silent. She had one great body on her, and she knew it. With nothing on but an orange thong and a Superman letter 'S' sticker covering each of her nipples, she knocked us off our feet by the way she posed.

Kat was the true animal in the studio, and she attacked the camera with her dazzling, eye-catching looks of beauty. She jumped out there with an outfit made with real paper currency. Kat's outfit was made with twenties, fifties, and one hundred dollar bills. She also had on a thong that was made from one hundred dollar bills. She killed it during her photo shoot.

Wet Wet made her move in front of the camera with an outfit made from bite-size pieces of Snickers bars. The candy only covered her breasts and her pussy lips. Everything else was out to be viewed.

Nikita Sunshine didn't play when she walked out in a pair of 8-inch black heels and a long, black, tight-fitting t-shirt that had rips and cuts all over it. Nikita Sunshine made me so happy with her look.

At last, it was Sweet Money Reds with the phat booty. She came out in a white Playboy bunny suit. She also had on the matching white bunny ears to go along with the outfit.

I was pleased with the photo shoot and couldn't wait to get the photos to one of the greatest graphic designers in the Washington metropolitan area, Oddball Designs. Oddball Designs does most of the book covers for publishers and self-published authors around the world. I knew they would add the right graphics to my pictures, and the business would come in like a homerun in the Major Leagues Association.

My cell phone rang, and it was my sweetheart, Envy. She wanted to take me out to dinner and share some special time together. I had no problem with that. I told Envy that I'd meet up with her in a couple hours. After hanging up, I sent the girls back to the massage parlor in cabs so they could get on top of that money again.

Envy and I met up at Twelve Restaurant and Lounge because she liked their food, and most of the time, there would be some sort of entertainment during the week. When I walked in the door, Envy was sitting at the bar having a drink of Grey Goose on the rocks.

"Hey, sweetheart, how are you feeling today?" I asked, while hugging her tightly.

"I'm fine, baby, I just wanted to see your face and be with the man I love so much. I love you, Dontaye, and nothing in this world will ever change that," Envy expressed, then kissed my lips.

I was so crazy in love with Envy, and I couldn't imagine my life without her. I believed her, and I knew she would never lie to me about anything.

We sat and talked about a lot of things. We promised we would never keep any secrets from each other. Envy asked me to share with her something that I hadn't told her yet, and she'd do the same. The only thing I hadn't shared with her was the fact that I ran an all-lesbian escort service. So, I decided to share it with her.

"Baby, I do have something that I need to share with you, but I'd rather show you than tell you about it. It will explain itself when you go there," I said as she looked me straight in the eyes.

"Why can't you just tell me? Is it a dangerous situation for me or you to be in?" she asked.

"No, sweetheart, not at all. I'll never put us in any danger."

Envy looked at me with concern. I knew it wouldn't be easy for her or me, but I felt if she was going to be my woman, than I should be honest and let her know what I do for a living.

After she had a few drinks, I was ready to take her to the massage parlor to see how she would digest it all. I didn't know if she was going to be jealous or if she was going to support my dreams of becoming one of the richest men in the game. I knew it could be a sensitive situation, and if I wasn't careful, it could come back to haunt me someday.

I got in my Benz, and she got in her all black 325i BMW. She followed me to the massage parlor, and after thirty-five minutes of driving, we were there. I parked in front of the door as she parked a couple cars behind my car. We walked up the steps, and as I opened the door, I looked in Envy's eyes. It looked like she couldn't believe what she was seeing.

The girls, who were glad that I was back, walked out to me with different messages of some sort or telling me about clients that they had serviced today. Envy didn't say a word. She just looked as if she had seen a ghost. I laughed for a second, and then I began to explain to her just how I made my money.

"My company is basically an escort service, but I promote it as an entertainment company that handles anything and everything under entertainment."

"I'm not understanding this. So you have females selling their bodies here?" Envy uttered.

"Well, yes, but we don't deal with men. It's an all-lesbian escort service that caters to only women and all of their sexual needs," I further explained.

"Wow, I have never seen or heard of anything like this. I respect your game, baby, and if I can be of any help, just let me know," she said as I continued to walk her through each of the massage rooms. "I find this to be amazing but shocking, Dontaye. I'm sure a lot of women will enjoy themselves as long as they are safe, though."

"Yes, we play safe around here. We keep everything sterile, and when needed, I buy brand-new toys and gadgets," I told her.

"Well, I'm behind you all the way," Envy said, then kissed me on the mouth before walking into the chat room.

"Now this is the sex chat room, where I charge $2.99 a minute to chat with my two most sexual women. One is dom and the other is a fem. And yes, they can make any woman bust a nut over and over again." I smiled.

"So you run this whole empire yourself, Dontaye?"

"Yes, I do, with the help of the girls, of course. We're a team in here," I said as we walked to my desk.

I had all of the girls to come and meet Envy so they would know who she was and get a chance to feel her out a little. Envy was glad to have met the girls, and she was even happier that I had shared my way of life with her as I moved upward to the top of the game.

Clients started coming in and the massage parlor was getting busier by the minute. So, I decided it was time to take Envy out somewhere while the girls kept their focus and made that money. After Envy and I left the massage parlor, I told her that I had some other business I needed to get on top of. So, I kissed her on the lips and told her that I'd call her later. She was cool about with it and agreed we should catch up later, but I noticed she still had a surprised look on her face.

Once I was in my car, I called my friend Boga Miller from my cell phone to see what he was up to at the moment. I really didn't want anything, but I was thinking about going out to see a local go-go band like Rare Essence or Backyard, two of the hottest bands in the Washington, D.C. area.

Chapter 19
WHAT THE HELL IS THAT?

B oga Miller and I went to see my favorite go-go band Rare Essence at the 123 Club on Georgia Avenue NW near Howard University. By the time we got to the club, the line was out the door and more than halfway down the block. We stood at the back of the line for a while because Rare Essence hadn't started the show yet, and I wanted to look over some of the beautiful young ladies. You never know who might show up.

"Dontaye, it's some bad bitches out here, man. I just got to book one of these gals. I need me a new female to chill with. I'm ready to cut my other female friend off. We're starting to argue a lot, and we can't agree on anything," Boga said as four young ladies walked up and stood behind us.

"Well, if the lines of communication are shutting down

between you and her, and all y'all do is argue, then I think you do need to meet some of these fine-ass honeys," I told him as I made a few steps forward in line.

Boga started talking to one of the four young women behind us. One of them looked familiar to me, so I decided to share some words with her.

"Hello, my name is Dontaye, and I just wanted to say you're one beautiful lady. And the skirt you're wearing looks so good on you. What's your name?" I asked.

"Why, thank you. My name is Cookie," the young woman responded.

"Cookie…that name fits you so well, because you look so sweet, baby," I uttered in a seductive way. "It seems as if I know you from somewhere. Have you ever been to the Delta Nightclub?" I questioned.

"Yeah. My sister dances there on Friday nights. MC Dom Diva is real close to my family, too. Do you know her?" Cookie asked.

"Do I know her? Yes, I know her. She works for me," I yelled out.

"She does? What kind of work does she do for you?" Cookie inquired.

"Well, let me ask you this. Have you ever heard of Big D Entertainment?"

144

"Yes, I have. I was at one of the clubs, and someone was talking about your company," Cookie said.

She then began telling me about herself and what she wanted to do in the entertainment business. She expressed her desire to write a book about being a groupie for most of the go-go bands in D.C. She said just as rap artists have groupies, so do local D.C. go-go bands. Her comment didn't surprise me. It was a new era, and people were doing whatever it took to get on the other side where the grass looked greener than the side they were already on. In most cases, they were fooled, but every now and then, the victim got lucky. Remember, the one who seeks greener grass always becomes the victim.

Before we knew it, we were standing at the front door about to be checked for weapons. I looked around and saw Boga and the young woman he was talking to walking back to the line where Cookie and I were standing. I could see a slight smirk on his face, as if he had done something and got away with it.

"Dontaye, this is Ransome. Ransome, this is Dontaye," Boga said, introducing us.

We got both Cookie and Ransome's contact numbers and told them that we would call them after the go-go.

"Man, them bitches are groupies. I just fucked Ransome in her car. We could see you and her friend Cookie from the car as we sat there," Boga told me.

"So how did you get to fuck her?" I asked.

Boga Miller pulled out a small bottle with some yellow liquid inside and showed it to me.

"What the hell is that?" I asked with curiosity.

"This is what they call Tweek. This shit will make any woman want to fuck in ten minutes. It's a love potion that they brew down in the country. You put this in a woman's drink, and the rest is history. You can fuck her brains out in ten minutes. Three old ladies sell this shit, and it works with no problem. They're not hip to it up here," he said, while putting the bottle back in his pocket.

Quickly, I thought about my girls at the massage parlor. I now felt like I couldn't trust Boga but so much around the girls. It's almost every man's dream to have sex with a lesbian, and I felt Boga Miller might be one of them.

As we made our way into the go-go establishment, Rare Essence was about to play. We went over to the bar and got a few drinks. I got a bottle of water, and Boga ordered Remy Martin with orange juice. About twenty minutes later, Rare Essence hit the stage, and they were on fire as usual.

While Boga and I made our way around the club, we saw numerous young ladies shaking their asses like the women in an Uncle Luke "Pop That Coochie" music video. A lot of young men were dancing freaky and up close on the females in the club. The women in D.C. really know how to shake what they got, not to mention they know how to use it. Being at the club gave me a new idea in marketing and promoting my girls at the massage parlor. I decided to give them a group name where everyone would recognize them all, and I would call them **THE NAUGHTY GIRLS.**

Chapter 20
GET IT THE WAY YOU CAN

I met up with my mother for a bite to eat. She began to tell me that she had been working on a tax scam that would put her in a very good position insofar as cash was concerned. As we both sat at a table near the back of the restaurant, Momma explained to me that she knew an African man that had a taxman that falsified tax documents. If we found some females who had children, and were strippers or on welfare, the taxman could falsify the tax documents so we could give the women one-thousand dollars from a six-thousand dollar hustle. She stated the government would never figure out what was going on because the strippers worked for themselves as entertainers, and there was a tax return for self-employed entertainers.

"I took three women to Gary, the guy that has the hookup

with the taxman, and everything worked out just fine. I made $6,000 out of the $18,000 that was returned from the three females," Rabbit said as we looked over the menu.

"Damn, Momma, that's one hell of a move there. Are you sure that won't come back to bite y'all in the ass?" I asked.

"Dontaye, you know how the Rabbit goes! I'm going to always try my hand. It's all about a hustle and not getting caught. I tell you this all the time. So, what's been going on with you?" Momma asked me as I took a drink from my glass of water.

"Everything has been good, but I do need to tell you something about someone that I let get close to me."

"Who's this person?"

"Momma, I met this female named Sugar Momma, and she's a drug dealer. She will kill anybody at the drop of a hat. I'm kinda paranoid and apprehensive about how I deal with her," I told her.

"Are you selling drugs?"

"No, Momma. She's a client, and she likes Wet Wet. One time while I was hanging out with her, a female named Solo shot out all of her car windows while I was in the car."

"Dontaye, I told you not to let people in your business, didn't I? Now you're going to find out how cruddy people are when you tell them your business."

"I know, Momma. I didn't want to tell you because I know what you always said about keeping people out your business," I said softly.

"Dontaye, that's the number one rule. If people don't know your business or what you're thinking, they don't know how to come at you. When people feel like they know you, they'll tell you what you want to hear to deceive you. Always remember that," Rabbit said.

After we placed our order for some honey barbeque wings, I told her about Sugar Momma and her beef with Solo. I couldn't tell her much about them personally, but I knew enough about the situation to know shit was going to get hectic.

"Fuck both of them bitches. I don't give a fuck about them. If either one of them bitches become a problem, just let me know. I don't have a problem with killing either one of them bitches when it comes to you," Momma voiced.

I also told Rabbit about my sex chat line service at the massage parlor. She laughed with admiration and told me it was a great idea.

"So what made you start up a sex chat line service?" she asked.

"You always told me to run a tight hustle game and to never be scared to take a risk in life. I will never forget the words you live by. NO GUTS NO GLORY! I'm making a lot of money

151

with the new service at the massage parlor. I'm going to hire about fifteen more people as soon as I open more lines. This will take my business to a whole new level."

"Dontaye, I'm so proud of you, son. Keep up the good work. Survive you must or die you will if you don't eat."

Since I had told her about all the other stuff going on in my life, I decided to tell her about Envy, too.

"So you met a bitch named Envy. What's up with that hoe?" Momma asked.

"I love Envy, Momma. She's cool, and I really like everything about her," I responded.

"Dontaye, what did 2Pac say in his records? Money over bitches, right?"

"But, Momma, what good is it to have money if you don't have anyone special in your life?" I whispered.

"Man, you run an all-lesbian escort service, and you're hung up on a hoe? Envy, huh? You got a lot to learn about these struggling-ass, lying-ass, do-anything-ass hoes. Women are sneaky; you can't trust them. You know I'm not telling you anything wrong."

"I know, Momma, but Envy's not like that. She's a good woman," I told Rabbit.

Momma laughed. "You've gotten weak at the zipper. That's the moment every hoe dreams of. The next thing you know she'll need rent money from you, her car note and insurance paid, and cash to get her hair and nails done. That's the sucker-ass game these hoes be pulling on weak-at-the-zipper niggas," Rabbit said.

I looked Momma in her eyes as she explained over and over the code to live by when dealing with a slick, struggling-ass woman, but the way I saw it, Envy would never carry it like that with me.

Chapter 21
A COLORFUL IMAGE IS A MUST

I started taking the Naughty Girls everywhere with me. We went to nightclubs, bars, strip clubs, movie theaters, restaurants, parties, modeling events, go-go spots, and we even shot our own commercial. I had to turn the word "image" into "reputation" at the same time. I knew that having a reputation would be my cornerstone of power, and with a colorful image, I could intimidate my enemies and win all together. Everything is judged by appearance. The unseen doesn't count. I had to make myself a magnet of attention by being more colorful and more mysterious, and the Naughty Girls was my way to being powerfully attractive.

Months passed, and my game had moved to another level. There was a big event going on at the D.C. Convention Center. Sonny Redz and Johnny Black were having a Players' Ball, and pimps from all over the world were invited. When I found out about it, I made it my business to be there with The Naughty Girls. The tickets sold for $2,500 a piece, and I had to pay for all eleven of the girls plus myself. So, I spent $30,000 in tickets easily and had no problem with it.

I took the Naughty Girls to Tysons Corner Mall to do their shopping. Most of the fems picked out Chanel outfits, while the doms and I decided on Giorgio Armani suits and shoes.

Two weeks had passed, and it was the day of the Players' Ball. At seven o'clock sharp the doors were opened to every pimp and hoe that could afford to be there. All you could see were limousines of every sort.

I saw this event as a good way to be seen and judged upon. This would be a great way to be talked about on an international level. The average pimp or hoe had never seen what they were about to witness in The Naughty Girls and me.

With the money I had spent in tickets, it put us in the VIP area. We had a private section and a table that sat twelve people. We were also served bottles of Moet, Grey Goose, and Remy Martin VSOP in a big ice-filled bowl. They also brought out a large platter of fried chicken wings and French fries. It was all good, because it was a pleasure to be in that spot, not to mention being entertained by the true legends in the pimpin' game.

Sonny Redz and Johnny Black hosted the event, and they were respected and recognized by every pimp in the building. As Sonny Redz spoke on the microphone, he acknowledged every pimp or player in the room.

"Good evening, pimps and players. As we know, this is a day of recognition, gratitude, acknowledgment, and respect, especially to those who respect the rules of the game and play by the rules of the game. If any player is going to knock a pimp for his hoe, then serve the nigga. If you hoes plan to choose another pimp, then break yourself, bitch," Sonny Redz said as the room full of pimps and hoes started clapping and yelling out in respect.

"That's right, pimp. Call it like it's supposed to be played, player!" one pimp yelled from his seat.

"Them outta pocket pimps and hoes need to be dealt with the old fashion way!" another pimp added.

"It's a new day, pimps, so don't play yourself outta pocket like a lot of the pimps have done before us. We have watched these brothers and sisters fall hard to the wayside. Remember that. So, be cool and be smart," Johnny Black said as everyone clapped again.

"It's now time to name the nominees for the Pimp of the Year Award. Let me see here. We have Pimpin' Tom from Florida, Pimpin' Jerome from Kansas, Pimpin' Ron from

Atlanta, Pimpin' Al from New York City, Pretty Toni from Saint Louis, and Pretty Shawn from Philadelphia. We have two female dom pimps up for the award this year, also. Let's give them a round of applause and show our respect," Sonny Redz said as he read the names from a long sheet of paper.

Each of the six pimps were handed the microphone so they could tell the judges why they should be Pimp of the Year. The judges would take notes about what each pimp said for consideration. Each pimp spoke for about twenty minutes before turning the microphone back over to Sonny Redz. I was all ears when each of the pimps got their chance to speak, because as they each gave up some knowledge, I got a lesson from their experiences in the game.

It wasn't long before it was time to announce the winner. Everyone seemed to have been waiting on the decision the judges made. Pimps and hoes were out of their seats and talking to fellow members of the game. Some had reminisced on the past either about some deaths that took place, money that was made, cars that were bought, or jewelry that had been purchased.

"Okay, pimps and hoes, here's the moment we all have been waiting for. It's time to show our appreciation for the real macaroni of the year. The one who made that money and kept them hoes in line. The one who looked the part, dressed the part, and played by all the rules when he or she was on the come up. The Pimp of the Year Award goes to Pretty Toni from Saint Louis, Missouri. Everybody give Pretty Toni a round of applause," Sonny Redz said, while handing Pretty Toni the microphone.

"I want to thank the judges for making the right decision, because I am the best above the rest, and I don't accept no less than five grand a night. Them bitches know I ain't to be fucked with when it comes to making my money. So, I got what my hand called for. It's every pimp's dream to be number one in the game. Thanks, and let's party!" Pretty Toni said, then she handed Sonny Redz the microphone.

Sonny Redz called me and the girls up to the stage.

"I want to introduce a special guest to everyone. I watched this young man grow up, and he runs a very unique stable. He does business in a way we all should have done it. This is my main man y'all—Dontaye."

Sonny Redz handed me the microphone.

"I'm Dontaye, and it was a great pleasure to be in the company of some true players. I heard and learned so much by just listening. Pretty Toni has much respect from me, and I want to say congratulations to you. I want to introduce everyone to my stable of girls. I call them The Naughty Girls. We do women only, and we put the lick down great," I said as every pimp and hoe applauded.

The DJ then started playing tracks from back in the early days of pimpin' and mixed in some up-to-date songs from rappers that speak of the pimp game, such as Nas, Jay-Z, and 50 Cent.

Chapter 22
ANYTHING A PERSON DOES ONCE, THEY'LL DO TWICE

I had just moved the rest of my personal belongings into Envy's place. We decided we should live together since things were getting serious between us. I felt we had the perfect relationship. We shared a lot of special moments, and the open communication lines were a key factor. Our sex life was the greatest. I would rate it one hundred out of one hundred. Our sex was the type of sex most people cheated on their mate to receive. So, basically, there would be no reason to seek any outside attention, if you know what I mean.

This newfound relationship that I had with Envy made me feel so bright and full of love inside. Everything I did with Envy, I always made it special. She loved seafood like most females, so I thought I'd surprise her one night and serve her one of my favorite seafood dishes, steamed lobster stuffed with crabmeat and shrimp.

On a Tuesday night just an hour before she got home, I steamed two lobsters along with one pound of shrimp. After steaming the lobsters and shrimp for about twenty minutes, I cut the shrimp into small pieces and mixed it with a pound of crabmeat and two raw eggs. I cut the back of the lobster tail straight down the back, opened it wide, and stuffed it with the mixture of the crabmeat, shrimp, and raw eggs. I then placed the two lobsters on a cookie sheet and put them in the oven broiler. Just as Envy walked in the door, I was pulling the stuffed lobsters out of the oven.

"Hey, baby," Envy said as she walked over and kissed my lips, while holding one yellow rose in her hand.

"Hey, sweetheart. I knew you'd be here soon, so I thought I would make something special for you."

"Oh, that's nice, honey," she replied as she put the yellow rose in a vase on the table.

For a minute, I thought she was going to hand the yellow rose to me, but she didn't. Instead, she headed for the bedroom, gathered her nightwear, and placed it in the bathroom.

I cut off all the lights in the house, then lit two candles and placed them in the candleholders on the table. We talked about our day over a candlelight dinner. I kissed Envy's hand as she began to tell me how her day went at the hospital.

"Honey, I had a long day today. They got butter from the duck," Envy said, speaking on how hard she had worked.

"Well, baby, if you want to quit, it's up to you. I'll take real good care of you. With my income, we can live well off of $40,000 a month," I told her, then put a fork full of crabmeat in my mouth as I waited for her to respond.

"I know, Dontaye, but I do need to keep my independence. I want to be able to help you if you ever need me. I'm not like them other women, the kind that's with you when you're up, but when you take a fall, those bitches leave you for the next man with some cash."

"I understand that, Envy, but I just want you to know that I'm a good man, and I got your back one hundred percent," I expressed as she leaned over the table and kissed me.

Enjoying the feeling inside, I kissed her back passionately.

As Envy sat back in her chair, she started to tell me about Doctor Crystal Wayne, her boss and good friend that she often hung out with at the hospital.

"Doctor Wayne bought me a Gucci watch and a handbag. She's real cool." Envy showed me the watch and the handbag.

I really didn't like the idea of her accepting gifts from the doctor, but I couldn't say anything about it. I had to keep my cool and act as if I was glad for her receiving such gifts.

"Doctor Wayne takes me out to lunch, too. She makes a lot of money, but the only thing is she has this young, stalking-ass husband. That dude is crazy. I'm really scared for her because of the way he sometimes yells and talks to her," Envy voiced with genuine concern.

"So how did you and her get so close? It's kind of odd for two women to just click like that, isn't it?" I asked.

Just then, her cell phone rang. Envy seemed to be a little agitated and disturbed when I asked that question, but she played if off when she answered her phone.

"Hello, Doctor Wayne. What up, young lady? I was just sitting here with Dontaye. He fixed us a stuffed lobster dinner, and we ate by candlelight. Wasn't that sweet of him?"

While she continued to talk, I gathered the dirty dishes and put them in the dishwasher. Although I was eavesdropping on Envy's conversation with Doctor Wayne and didn't hear anything suspicious being said, I just couldn't make myself accepting her friendship with the bitch. I got the feeling that there would be some slick shit going down in the future. I heard all about the shit that takes place in those hospitals. Everything from men fucking women in mop closets to bitches cheating on her nigga with the doctor she worked for at the hospital. Momma always told me not to let a woman's pussy get me whipped, but in this case, I was in love, and pussy was just half

164

the problem. This shit I had for Envy was mental.

The next morning, I decided I would go purchase a few things for Envy to show her that I could buy her expensive things, as well. I may not be a doctor, but I make just as much money as they do, if not more.

I stopped at the massage parlor and got about $10,000 so I could go all out for Envy. I started at Tysons Corner. I bought her everything from Gucci boots, Gucci tennis shoes, Gucci dresses, and Gucci suits. I wasn't playing any games. I wanted my woman to clearly see that she had a man that would go beyond the usual limits to prove his loyalty and show just how special she was to me. The next thing I did was hit every store on Wisconsin Avenue. I purchased so many clothes and shoes for Envy that I was sure to get her attention.

Somehow after living with Envy for months, I began realizing that I was now in competition with Doctor Wayne for Envy's love and friendship. This was a glimpse of what Rabbit was trying to tell me in the very beginning, but now it was too late. My heart was already involved, and my inner passion for her was now clashing with my ego. My days had started to depend on how Envy's moods were, whether they were good or bad, or whether her drive would be aimless. I totally took the focus off me, and it became all about her—something that would eventually take me out the frame.

I found myself tree boxing on Envy. Most people call it spying. I would follow her to and from work in different cars to see if she was cheating on me. I would meet people in the hospital where she worked and pay them to tell me if she was fucking someone who worked there. A few people told me that she had been running around with a guy who worked in the cafeteria, and that didn't sound good at all. I must admit I had it bad, and her hanging with Doctor Wayne was not making my relationship with Envy any better.

Even though I slept beside Envy every night, I began to feel distance between us, as if someone else was in the picture. Or it could have been more like someone was in her ear when I wasn't around, because I noticed changes in her attitude slightly. She started talking sassy and was snappy at me sometimes. All these things were signs that usually appeared when a woman had met someone else. When that type of attitude begins, it's evident that someone is controlling the woman's thoughts and your household from the outside. I decided that I would talk to Envy about my feelings in hopes that she could reassure me that I had nothing to worry about in our relationship.

A few days later, I sat down next to Envy on the loveseat in the living room and spilled my inner feelings to her.

"Sweetheart, I love the ground you walk on. Ain't nothing

166

in this world that I wouldn't do to make you happy," I started.

"Awww, Dontaye, that's so sweet of you to say. I love you, too," Envy claimed.

"But, honey, there are some things I want to ask you."

"Okay. What's going on?" Envy asked.

"Are you cheating on me? The reason I'm asking you is because my friends that work at the hospital tell me that you be having men come in your office to have sex with you. What's up with that?" I asked nervously.

"Dontaye, the only person I want is you. Don't believe that shit. If I wanted to be with someone else, I would tell you," she told me, while rubbing my hands.

Even though she said she wasn't interested in anyone but me, I still felt doubtful and suspicious because I had also noticed that she had been telling me lies about certain things in the past. At that point, I didn't know what to think. My head and my heart were at war with concerns of another man fucking my woman.

Conflicted, I started sucking Envy's pussy on the spot, trying to take my mind off the possibility that my woman was fucking with someone else. I licked and sucked on her clitoral hood for a while before I started down to her clitoris. She held my head and guided my mouth to the perfect place. Once I was in the right position, I straight tongue fucked her like it was my penis. I started licking around her anal opening as I stuck my middle finger in and out of her vaginal hole. I licked alongside her labia majora to the other side of her labia minora. I would always do my best to please Envy, because I loved to hear her scream from the pleasure she received from me.

I sucked Envy's pussy until she creamed several times, and my chin was wet from her warm juices. After I sucked on her pussy for another twenty minutes, I opened my zipper, pulled my big dick out, and slammed it into her awaiting wet mouth. I began to put a hurting on her mouth like I had slaughter her hot, warm pussy. I fucked Envy's mouth hard before I told her to bend over and let me fuck that pussy from the back.

After a good hour and a half, my work was done. I released so much cum in her pussy that it started running down her right leg.

"Wow," is all I could say as we laid on the floor and fell fast asleep.

Chapter 23
IT WAS WRITTEN THAT WAY

Boga Miller and I went out to Twelve Lounge so I could try to clear my mind a bit. The shit I'd been taking myself through over the last few weeks had been very strenuous on my mind. I really don't drink alcohol, but on this night, I really needed to be under a mind-altering substance. So, I sat at the bar with Boga and told the bartender to bring me a double shot of Grey Goose vodka with a hit of cranberry juice. After the bartender made my drink, he asked if I wanted to run a tab. I said to myself, *What the hell. I don't really drink, so I guess I could drink a few more.* With my mind made up, I told the bartender to start a tab. I bought Boga a few drinks as we sat and discussed some of my thoughts and plans for the upcoming weeks.

Bike week was coming up in South Carolina, and my plan

was to be there with the Naughty Girls, promoting them as models and promoting my Big D Entertainment. It wouldn't hurt to promote the massage parlor, as well.

Boga Miller was coming along just fine as an assistant. The only thing I didn't like about him was that he would pour that sex potion Tweek in every woman's drink he came in contact with, and that's not good. I got too much to lose to get caught up in some date rape bullshit. At some point, I planned to slow him down and get him to understand that he didn't need to use that shit on women. They were chasing dick and pussy like there wasn't going to be any tomorrows. So, what was the need for it?

All I really needed Boga to do was drive me around, hold a pistol, if need be, and be down for whatever with me if any drama went down. The work wasn't hard.

An hour had passed, and I received a call from Lil' Porsche. I hadn't heard from her in a while, but I was glad to hear from her.

"Hey, stranger, how have you been?" I inquired when I answered my cell phone.

"Hey, Dontaye, how are you? I've been meaning to call you, but I've been real busy with going in and out of town and hitting up club after club while doing my thing. You feel me? My CD is getting major play on the radio and the clubs are feeling it. People come up to me all the time asking for autographs," Lil' Porsche shared with excitement.

"That's good. I'm glad to hear that everything is moving to another level and that the picture is getting bigger for you. Next there will be news and entertainment interviews. After that, the paparazzi will be chasing you down everywhere. Your future looks good, young lady." I said.

"I'll be performing at the Miss Soft and Wet competition during Gay Pride. Mz. Vicki called me a few days ago and told me that she has three events that she wants me to perform at. That's what's up," Lil' Porsche said as I gulped down the last of my drink.

"So where are the events going to be held?" I asked.

"Oh yeah, let me tell you where. I will be here in Washington, D.C. at Club Wet. After that, I'll be in Atlanta at the Rainbow Club, and then I'll be in Miami at the Razzle Dazzle Club," she told me.

"Well, I want to be there. Make sure you keep me posted on all the events so I can be there with The Naughty Girls."

"The Naughty Girls? Who in the hell is that?" Lil' Porsche asked.

I had to explain to her what my drop was in the game, so to make things easy, I just brought her up to speed with my hustle game.

"I have an escort service under my entertainment company, as well, and they're the ones with all the talent at the massage parlor, if you know what I mean," I said as I switched my cell phone to my left ear.

"Oh wow, that's what's up. I like that, Dontaye. So I can come through and get my carpet munched on? I love myself some motherfucking head, damn!" Lil' Porsche yelled out with inspiration.

"If that means you want to cum, then yes, the girls will be more than glad to fuck you. One day real soon, I want you to come to the massage parlor and enjoy the sessions, if you can handle the action," I said, while she laughed on the other end of the phone.

I told Lil' Porsche that I would give her a call later because I wanted to pay the bartender and get back to the massage parlor.

As Boga Miller and I got in my car and pulled off, I could see the looks on people's faces as they admired my Mercedes Benz. I looked back at them with a look that said, *I know I got a fly-ass car.*

With Bike Week and Gay Pride quickly approaching, I decided to take some of the girls' pictures from the last photo shoot and have Davida at Oddball Designs create the graphics behind the photos and make calendars, posters, keychains, T-shirts, and buttons.

As we made our way back to the massage parlor, Boga started telling me some stories about his teen years down in the country.

"Man, I remember when I was in high school, and we use to fuck all the girls off that Tweek. Even the doms fucked a lot of women at the clubs with that Tweek juice. It was ten doms in my hood that ran a train on this fem for about fifteen hours. The broad had been fucked every type of way possible. She had her pussy sucked and fucked all that she could that day. I filmed the sexcapade and tried to upload it on YouTube, but it wouldn't accept it because of the explicit sex footage," he told me.

I couldn't believe they were doing that type of shit in the country more than ten years ago. I guess sex is just as addictive as any legal or illegal drug. People will get it any way they can, just like a junkie.

Boga talked about members of his family in the country who had kids together, like second and third cousins. The more he talked, the more I understood why he's the way he is with that liquid sex potion, Tweek.

Just before we got to the massage parlor, I received a phone call from Wet Wet. She was crying and yelling so much that I couldn't understand what she was trying to tell me.

"Wet Wet, slow down, baby, and tell me what's going on. Calm down, That's right. Calm down. Now tell me what happened," I said.

"Rainbow was just killed at her grandmother's house. She was double parked in front of her grandmother's door, and a car full of young boys was being chased by the police. They ran into the back of her grandmother's car, breaking Rainbow's neck. She died at the scene of the accident," Wet Wet cried.

Immediately, I went over to Rainbow's grandmother's house, and like Wet Wet said, Rainbow had died at the scene. Her body was still slumped over the steering wheel of her grandmother's old 1966 Ford Mustang. The paramedics began pulling Rainbow's lifeless body out of the car shortly after I got there. I didn't get a chance to speak with her grandmother because some neighbors had taken her away from the house so she wouldn't suffer another heart attack or stroke from the stress of her granddaughter's death.

The next door neighbor told me that Rainbow's mother had died the same way, on the same day, on that same block, in the same place, about the same time, twenty years earlier when Rainbow was just a child.

I was fucked up about Rainbow's sudden death. Wet Wet really took it hard being that they were in a close relationship, and the rest of the girls were just as sad.

About a week later, Rainbow's funeral was held at Pope Funeral Home right off of Minnesota Avenue SE. There were so many people at her funeral. Not only was she loved by us, but she was also loved by many people in the life, as well.

WE ALL LOVE YOU, RAINBOW.

Chapter 24

BEAUTIFUL THINGS ARE SOMETIMES ILL

Weeks passed, and I noticed that Envy had switched totally up on me. The very things that she'd never do in the beginning were now the things she did on the regular basis. Suddenly, she was coming up missing and not answering my telephone calls when she was at work. During the last couple months, it seemed as if my being at her place started drawing us apart instead of bringing us closer together. The arguing, the fighting, and the name calling had all played a major role in our now distant affair. I never thought it would go down like this, and I never thought her love for me would just change so quickly. The fucked up part about all of it was that I couldn't shake the deep feelings I had inside for her. If Envy was just a regular woman I had met somewhere on a job or something, I could have just fucked her and roll, but that wasn't the case. I fell in love with her from day one—something I was taught never to do. I didn't feel the need to hold back my feelings or be careful about how I dealt with her. It was all about my devotion to her.

Now, I must admit that she was a sweetheart once you got to know her, and I had a weakness for her smile, her love, and the way she made me melt like butter whenever she brought me to an orgasm. No woman had ever done that to me ever.

Even though Envy hadn't come home for about a week, I still stayed at her place during those long, lonely nights. As I sat on the bed that Thursday night watching television, I heard the front door locks turn as if someone was coming into the house. I looked from the bedroom and saw that it was Envy. Although I was both angry and hurt deep down inside, my animosity had changed when I saw her beautiful face.

"Envy, I miss you, baby. Please come back home," I said with a harmless tone.

"I will, Dontaye. I just need my space for a while. I don't like the fighting that's going on between us. I have enough shit on my mind. I don't need any extra shit," she replied as she turned on the shower.

"So where have you been staying?" I asked softly.

"Dontaye, are we going to go through more arguing right now? If I wanted you to know where I was, I would've called you, right?" Envy said, then closed the bathroom door.

Now, I'm not the type of man to hit women, but the shit she was saying was killing me inside. Still, I knew I had to control my ego, because if I hadn't, she would've gotten her ass whooped a long time ago. She had gotten into the habit of calling me all types of disrespectful names whenever we got into a petty argument. That alone should have been gotten her a serious smackdown. For real! Not wanting to get into another argument, I decided I would leave and give her the space she wanted since it was her apartment that I was staying in.

Before Envy got out the shower, though, I pulled out a small tape recorder from my dresser drawer, pressed record, and threw it under the bed so I could hear her every conversation after I left the house. When Envy exited the bathroom, I told her that I was going to my mother's place to chill and think some things over. She just looked at me as if she hadn't heard a word I said.

I walked out the front door, got in my car, and pulled off. I didn't want to face Rabbit with my drama. She had warned me that this shit was sure to happen, and I didn't want to hear the things she would have to say about my situation with Envy. So, I went to the massage parlor and laid low for the next three days before returning to Envy's place.

On Monday of the next week, I went back to Envy's house

179

about twelve o'clock noon only to find the small tape recorder I had left was full of secrets that Envy concealed like a deadly weapon. I rewound the recorder back to the very beginning, and it seemed as if she made a call as soon as I left out the front door.

"Damn, I like the way you eat my pussy, you short, built-to-the-ground, no-teeth motherfucka. I wish you could come over here right now and suck my ass and lick all up in this juicy, wet, throbbing pussy. Your long fat dick really does a number on my pussy when you longstroke me from the side, baby. You got to take it easy on me if you want to still hit this pussy with that big-ass dick. It hurts my pussy when you get to banging and beating it up," Envy said at the beginning of the tape.

Then she started telling the person how she loved me and wasn't trying to end our relationship, but at the same time, she wanted to continue being with them. I could hear Envy tell the guy that she was going to brush her teeth and call him back. Fifteen minutes of tape went silent, but then it picked up as Envy dialed the person back.

"Hey, baby, what's that tongue doing over there? Why don't you drive over here and stick it all up in my pussy so I can go to sleep."

Envy laughed to the response of the person on the other end of the telephone. I heard her tell the guy that she wanted him to meet her at a particular restaurant on 13th and K Street Northwest at 6:30 p.m. on Saturday.

So, I waited for Saturday, and you can bet your bottom dollar that I was on 13th and K Street NW on that day and time. I sat over in Franklin Park with a pair of binoculars to watch for Envy and her secret lover. After I sat for about ten minutes, I saw her from a distance with a brown skin guy that stood about 5'11" tall with a bush. The guy had his arm around Envy as they sat in front of the restaurant to eat. My heart dropped as I sat there in disbelief with an uncontrollable urge to kill the person that was meeting my woman in secret places. I had to understand that Envy was just as guilty as the guy, if not guiltier.

Having seen all that I needed to see at this point, my emotions nor my ego could take no more. I got up and took a long, lonely walk to my car, which seemed to take me forever to get in. I quickly went back to Envy's house with a different tape recorder. This one was voice activated and would only record when someone began to talk in the room. I turned it on and threw the new recorder under her bed once again.

Since Envy wanted to play games with me, I started to make plans on how I would bring her bullshit to an end and make her see just who the fuck she was playing with. The shit she was doing to me was the very same shit women do to other men, which normally resulted in a domestic violence court case for a motherfucker.

I had bought the bitch diamond rings, a diamond watch, more than $10,000 worth of clothes, and most of all, I broke rule number 1 - **NEVER TRUST A BITCH!**

Two days later, I found myself drunk and hiding from my own self in a Days Inn Hotel off Route 50 in New Carrollton, Maryland. My love for Envy was breaking me down to my lowest point, and I didn't know how to deal with it. It seemed as if my thoughts were beginning to get crazy, and due to my abysmal thinking, nothing was clear to me. I didn't remember anything. I totally forgot I had a business, money, a car, and I even forgot about The Naughty Girls. I must have been comatose.

Days later, after I pulled myself together, I was back and out for revenge.

"Fuck her and the nigga she's fuckin'. I got something for both of their asses. Bitch, you want to cheat on me with another man after all the things I provided you with?! Okay, bitch, I got you," I mumbled to myself.

I went back to Envy's house with my Glock-9 semi automatic pistol, and my ego had me ready to commit a murder. Just as I got to her house, I saw Envy and the same guy with the bush that she was at the restaurant with on 13th and K Streets.

182

They were walking in the doorway of her house. *This bitch is a real risk taker,* I thought to myself. *She actually brought the muthafucka to the house. WOW!*

I couldn't believe what I was witnessing. Suddenly, anger got the best of me, and I couldn't take any more at that point.

I walked around to the side of the house and climbed through the bathroom window on the first floor. I figured if they went there to fuck, they wouldn't hear me if I got in the house through the lower-level bathroom.

When I got into the house, I could hear a lot of heavy breathing. The bed was squeaking rapidly with every second that went by. As I slowly crept up the stairs, I began to hear the sexual sounds of pleasure as they became increasingly louder while they indulged intensely in sexual intercourse. When I reached the bedroom doorway, I saw both of them asshole naked.

With not a stitch of clothing on, Envy was laid back on the bed with her legs held wide open and both eyes closed. The motherfucker she brought to the house was face down in her pussy just licking and sucking away on her long clitoris like a professional pussy muncher.

I sat down on the floor with the pistol in my hand and watched as they were getting it in. After fucking Envy with his tongue for twenty minutes, the dude positioned his ass over top of Envy's face, and she started licking away.

"Damn, baby, suck it. That's right. Give me that crucial head, love. I want it just like that. You know what to do," the dude coached.

As Envy gave the person oral sex, I couldn't bear to watch them any longer.

"Bitch muthafucka, get off my woman before I blow your gotdamn brains out!" I yelled.

The person jumped up off the bed and turned to me as Envy rolled off the bed with the covers wrapped around her body.

"Baby, what are you doing with that gun? Please don't shoot us. I'm sorry, Dontaye," Envy cried.

I pointed the pistol at both of them, moving it from left to right. All types of things were running through my mind. Thoughts of seeing my dad as a homosexual and a male prostitute, my mother as a hardcore lesbian dyke, classmates teasing me about my parents, and all types of hang-ups with anger just burst through my veins. I was ready to explode with the inner fire that was burning my soul.

When I looked at the person Envy was with, I was ready to start shooting. With my finger on the trigger and the pistol to his head, that's when I noticed I was looking at a woman. She had nice, perky breasts like a teenager, a beautiful face, and as I took a closer look down at her body, I noticed she had a small-like penis and a vaginal hole, too.

"Open your legs, muthafucker!" I shouted as I began to blackout with anger.

I looked down closer, and just as I thought, it was a hermaphrodite. At that point, I went fuckin' crazy. I blacked the fuck out, and all I heard was the sound of rapid gunfire from my 9mm semi-automatic handgun. I was there to repay that bitch for my pain.

TO BE CONTINUED...
FIND OUT WHAT HAPPENS NEXT FROM ENVY'S SIDE

CPSIA information can be obtained
at www.ICGtesting.com
Printed in the USA
FFOW03n0421190815
16088FF